He studied her critically.

'At the risk of seeming to criticise your taste in clothes, you don't seem to be suitably attired to prepare dinner for three hungry males.'

'Probably because I haven't the slightest intention of doing so. Cordon bleu cookery wasn't part of my training. Perhaps things were different in your day, Dr Harris.' Her tone was deceptively sweet.

The remarkable eyes narrowed abruptly. Then he laughed. 'Dr Whittaker, I presume?'

Dear Reader

Caroline Anderson gives us the final part of her trilogy, KNAVE OF HEARTS, where Anne meets her Jake again after eight years—a tearjerker! OUT OF PRACTICE is Lynne Collins's fortieth book for the medical series, and it is a lovely story set in general practice. I know you will enjoy it. Margaret O'Neill's hero, Rupert, is touchingly protective of Toni, and, to round off, Sheila Danton takes us to India, with all that country's problems and joys. See you next month. . .

The Editor

Lynne Collins's many Medical Romances are based on personal experience of hospital life, backed by research and information from her many medical friends in the Medical profession. She likes writing about hospital settings for their wealth of human interest. Married with one son, she now lives on the Essex coast, and enjoys travel, meeting people, talking, walking and gardening.

Recent titles by the same author:

HEART IN CRISIS
REPENTANT ANGEL

OUT OF PRACTICE

BY

LYNNE COLLINS

MILLS & BOON LIMITED
ETON HOUSE 18–24 PARADISE ROAD
RICHMOND SURREY TW9 1SR

First published in Great Britain 1992
by Mills & Boon Limited

This edition 1993

ISBN 0 263 77997 1

Set in 10½ on 12 pt Linotron Times
03-9302-47284

Typeset in Great Britain by Centracet, Cambridge
Made and printed in Great Britain

CHAPTER ONE

A SMUDGE of weariness etched striking sapphire eyes in the pretty oval of a youthful face, and Laurie sighed as she lifted the heavy mass of richly dark curls from her neck and shoulders with shapely hands, the unconsciously graceful gesture tautening the cool cotton shirt across her pert breasts.

After her long drive from London along a motorway plagued with roadworks, she felt hot and tired and not at all sure that it had been wise to turn her back on Hartlake and Cris and all her friends for a new venture and a new home in rural Sussex. No one had appeared in response to her repeated pressing of the doorbell, and she wondered if its peal had been heard at all in the distant regions of the surprisingly large house.

The heavy front door stood wide, an invitation to enter, and Laurie picked up her case and took a tentative step into the shadowy hall with its high, ornate ceiling, black and white square-tiled floor and sweeping staircase, relics of a former grandeur and a more romantic age.

'Anyone home?'

Umber House was cool and still and somehow welcoming in spite of its silence, and some of the tensions of the long day ebbed away as she looked about her with growing approval.

Somewhere, a door banged, a welcome sign of life. Once more she heard the alerting bark of a dog that emanated from the back of the house. Wondering if she should explore further in search of life in human form, Laurie studied an ancient oil painting of three little girls in crinolines who played with a prancing wolfhound against a background of a country house much like the one in which she stood.

'A dog is much more reliable than a doorbell, fortunately. I hope you haven't been standing there for the past half-hour.'

At the sound of the deep, apologetic tones, she turned to see a broad-shouldered, long-limbed stranger who was soberly grey-suited in spite of the heat of the midsummer day. 'Only a few minutes. The bell doesn't work, then? I did try it—several times.'

'I'm sure you did.' His smile was warm but fleeting, slightly absent. 'I'm very glad to see you, anyway. You're so late that we thought you'd changed your mind about helping us out.'

'I thought I'd made pretty good time, actually,' said Laurie.

He was very tall, very well put together, with wide shoulders and narrow hips, auburn hair aflame in a shaft of sunlight from a high window and piercing blue eyes dominating a lean, craggy face with their keen intelligence and hint of humour. It was an interesting face, and he was a handsome man, so attractive that Laurie felt a slight shock of interest that surprised her. For he was nothing like Cris, fair of hair and face and stocky in build, with Celtic good looks that had awakened her long-dormant emotions.

Meeting the penetratingly perceptive eyes, Laurie knew he was well aware of his impact on women, and her own unexpected reaction to his striking good looks and powerful physique. She was instantly on the defensive as an unwelcome, give-away warmth crept into her face.

'We expected you some time this morning—but never mind. I'll show you the kitchen and you can make yourself some tea before you settle in. I'll have to leave you to it, however.' He shot a glance at the expensive gold watch on a narrow, bronzed wrist. 'I was about to leave for the surgery when I heard Angelo barking. . .'

Enlightened, although she had already guessed his identity, Laurie held out her hand with an assured smile. 'Dr Harris, I presume?'

Like many doctors, he had little time to spare for the social niceties, she thought wryly, as he ignored both smile and outstretched hand to hustle her through a door and along a stone-flagged corridor. He was rushed rather than rude, she decided charitably.

He threw open the door of a vast, untidy room, a sunny, well-equipped kitchen that needed an organising hand. 'The place is a mess,' he announced without apology. 'We've had a measles epidemic on our hands on top of everything else, so there hasn't been much time for the chores. Can I ask you to do the laundry and restock the freezer this afternoon, if nothing else? I've left a list and some money, and you'll find a supermarket in the village. Jamie will be home about half-three, wanting something to eat—a neighbour drops him off from school. . .' He broke off as he saw her startled expression. 'I believe my partner explained the set-up?'

Laurie looked at the overflowing laundry basket, at dishes piled in the sink and at a floor that badly needed to be swept and scrubbed. 'I'm not at all sure now that I understood the set-up,' she said drily.

He appeared not to notice the acid tone. 'Get Edward to explain more fully when he comes in. He's doing some house calls but should be home soon. I'm sorry to dump this lot on you and run, but a doctor's life isn't his own, as you know. I'm sure you'll cope. You look like a capable girl!'

In no mood to appreciate the compliment in his tone or the charm of a sudden, blazing smile, Laurie glowered as the door closed on him—and he returned unexpectedly to catch the full force of her glare as he put his handsome head back into the room.

'Oh, by the way, we've given you the Blue Room. First floor, end of the corridor. I've put out linen for the beds. . .'

Then he really had gone, in a rush, leaving Laurie to fume. For this wasn't the welcome she had expected, with Edward out on rounds and Judd Harris treating her like a wardmaid! She cursed her cousin's characteristic vagueness and her own haste to escape that had led her into a situation where she was apparently expected to run the household as well as help out with a busy practice!

Resisting the temptation to drive straight back to the city and her cosy flat, she mounted the grand sweep of the staircase to vet her room. Expecting the worst, she was pleasantly surprised, in spite of the unmade bed and dusty surfaces. Large and bright and comfortably furnished, it had its own small but adequate bathroom, and that was a bonus, for Laurie had felt doubtful about sharing with two men, even if one *was* cousin and friend and lifelong confidant.

Cheerful chintz curtains hung at long windows overlooking a rambling but well-kept garden that she admired as she knelt on the chintz-cushioned window-seat.

A dog loped across the lawn, a rangy wolfhound like the one in the painting but looking friendlier than his size and breed implied. Nevertheless, Laurie hoped Edward would be home to introduce them before she encountered the animal who might assume her to be an intruder.

She felt rather like an intruder in this tranquil and very lovely setting, a far cry from the wards and operating theatres and crowded clinics where she had daily dealt with the problems of inner-city deprivation and depression. She hoped the years at Hartlake hadn't hardened her, but she had been compelled to acquire a second and tougher skin to cope with some of her experiences. At times she might have seemed uncaring, when in fact she cared too much and allowed things to get her down.

The needless death of a tiny patient had left her feeling very down and vulnerable to the unexpected attentions of Crispin Page, a senior surgical registrar at Hartlake with a reputation as a heartbreaker, a string of conquests to his credit. She had been foolishly flattered by his interest, bowled over by his charm and gulled into believing that he really cared about her.

The passionate pursuit of a determined man had swept the usually cautious Laurie into love before she knew it, but a serious relationship had never been on the cards for Cris. He'd hurt her badly, and she had felt the need to escape from Hartlake and the daily torment of encountering him as well as the silent sympathy of colleagues.

That was the worst of falling for someone in the same profession, she thought wryly as she unpacked, storing her clothes in the roomy wardrobe and chest, stamping her personality on the room with familiar trifles, books and photographs. She'd take care not to make that mistake again! In any case, she meant to concentrate on medicine in future and forget about love and the heartache it could bring.

Edward's offer had come at just the right time, and Laurie was looking forward to working with her cousin in his country practice. It would certainly be different from the demanding life of a hospital paediatrician, and Edward had hinted at the possibility of a partnership at the end of her six–month commitment. She thought it unlikely that she would want to spend the rest of her life in a small country town. But one never knew.

She had little idea what the coming months had in store for her, but she hadn't bargained for someone like Judd Harris with his disconcerting impact on her unsuspecting senses. He was too attractive for comfort, with those intensely blue eyes and that oddly disarming smile.

Unpacking finished, she turned her thoughts to the pile of dirty dishes in the kitchen sink and the heap of unwashed laundry, and knew that, while she might resent the tasks thrust upon her so unceremoniously, she couldn't continue to ignore them. It would be a poor beginning if she allowed Edward to return from his house calls to such chaos! Moreover, the afternoon was now well advanced and Jamie, whoever he might be, would soon be home—and she hadn't even *looked* at the shopping list that Judd had so obligingly left for her!

Well, she might be just as capable as he had assumed, but she wasn't Superwoman, Laurie told herself as she surveyed the disorder. Shopping would have to wait and a presumably hungry child would have to be content with whatever she could find in fridge or larder.

'Hello. Are you the new one? We've had three already. Can I have some bread and jam, please?'

Laurie turned from sorting laundry to smile at the little boy who stood just inside the garden door. She liked children, and he was a particularly appealing specimen, a miniature edition of her new colleague, with his crop of bright auburn hair, sturdy and promising to be tall, keen blue eyes in an eager, good-looking face—and a rather lordly manner!

'I hope to give you something more substantial than that for tea once I've investigated the fridge,' she told him lightly, wondering why Edward had failed to mention his partner's small son—and if Jamie's mother also lived at Umber House. If so, why didn't *she* do the washing and stock the freezer?

'It isn't for me. It's for Angelo. . .' At the mention of his name, sharp ears pricked and the dog hurtled across the lawn and into the house to thrust a wet nose into the boy's hand, snuffling. 'He likes bread and jam.'

'That probably expains why he wasn't anxious to take a bite out of me,' Laurie smiled. She had made friends with the sentimental, overgrown puppy who would no doubt greet a masked burglar with the same degree of delight in his bark and the thrash of his long tail. It was certainly the only welcome she'd received so far! 'But it doesn't seem a very healthy diet for a dog.'

'He likes it,' Jamie insisted. 'Where's Dad?'

'Apparently he had a surgery this afternoon,' she told him.

'I forgot. I wanted to go fishing. Do you like fishing?' His small face brightened with hope. 'We have our own river at the end of the garden with lots of fish in it.'

Laurie recalled the gleaming ribbon of sunlight reflecting on water that wove between tall trees that she had glimpsed from her bedroom window. 'That must be fun.' Closing the door of the loaded washing-machine, she frowned at the unfamiliar symbols.

'I have to be careful. I'm not allowed to play at the water on my own.' Jamie studied her for a reflective moment. 'I do, though,' he confided on an impulsive burst of trust.

Before she could frame a reply, a tall, fair-haired girl hurried in and spun Jamie round to face her with a snatch at his small shoulders. 'Why didn't you wait, you naughty boy? You know you're supposed to wait for me no matter how late I am! I was really worried, until Kay said you'd walked home with some older children. . .'

'I like to walk. I was all right. Angelo met me.' Tone and attitude were defiantly stubborn.

'I do wish you wouldn't make life difficult, Jamie. . .' The girl sighed and shook her head. 'Kids!' she deplored light-heartedly, shafting a rueful smile at the startled Laurie, who wasn't at all sure of the situation. 'Sorry to burst in on you—I should introduce myself, shouldn't I? Patsy Meridew. I live just up the hill, and Jamie goes to the same school as my little girl. I've an arrangement with Judd—Dr Harris—to collect him and bring him home. I expect he told you. But Jamie doesn't always wait—he's so independent!' She ruffled Jamie's hair and he jerked from her touch, scowling. She smiled, not minding the rebuff, and urged lightly, 'Go outside and play with Kay, Jamie.'

Boy and dog bounded from the room and Patsy perched a shapely bottom in bright, tight jeans on a kitchen stool and produced cigarettes from her capacious bag. Laurie shook her head to the offer, longing to point out that she would rather the girl didn't smoke in the kitchen. Or at all, for that matter. She had seen too many patients with lung damage and cardio-vascular disease caused by cigarettes.

'Jamie doesn't like me,' Patsy declared blithely. 'Thinks I've got designs on his dad.' She laughed and blew a perfect smoke-ring. 'Who wouldn't have? He's gorgeous, isn't he? By the way, it's number six, if that's normal washing—socks and shirts and underwear,' she went on helpfully. 'It's the one I use when I help out between housekeepers. That's a foreign machine—looks complicated but isn't once you get used to it.'

'Thanks.' Laurie turned the dial and switched on the machine, a little at a loss and wishing Edward would come home and take charge. She glanced through the kitchen window. The children weren't playing together. In grey shorts and shirt that resembled his father's sober suiting, Jamie was digging holes in the lawn with a sharp-pointed stick, looking bored and slightly sullen. The little girl was trying to clamber on to Angelo's reluctant back, an obvious tomboy in spite of the frills and furbelows on her frock. 'How old is Kay?' she asked, trying to introduce some normality into an Alice-in-Wonderland whirl of events.

'Six—a few weeks younger than Jamie. I left her father before she was born. He was playing around, and I wasn't having that. He's never seen her, isn't interested. Men can be bastards, can't they?'

Patsy's bright tone shrugged off the past with an ease that Laurie envied. But six years was a long time. Perhaps one day she would be so insouciant about the pain of loving and losing Cris. 'Some men,' she agreed carefully.

Patsy shot her an amused glance. 'Sounds as if

you retain some illusions! Well, why not? Even I think that one day I'll meet a man who isn't only interested in getting me between the sheets. It isn't easy for a woman on her own with a kid, is it?' She stubbed her half-smoked cigarette. 'If you're making tea, I'd love a cup. It's so hot, and I've been on the go all day. I'll put the kettle on, shall I?'

She was quicksilver, darting to seize the bright red kettle jug and fill it at the tap, plugging it in before scooping mugs from a wooden tree, finding tea-bags and sugar and swooping on the fridge for milk, so much at home that she had to be a regular visitor, Laurie felt, wondering if the pretty neighbour did indeed have designs on the good-looking Judd Harris.

She spoke as if he was available. So where was Jamie's mother? Dead? Divorced? Or did they have one of those amicable arrangements that allowed them both to follow their fancies? Recalling a warm mouth and a brief but stunning smile, the undeniable magnetism of the man, Laurie could believe that the GP spent much of his time fighting off the Patsy Meridews of the neighbourhood. Or *not*, perhaps.

'Do you take sugar? I *shouldn't*, I know. I'm far too fat. . .' Patsy ran complacent hands over a trim stomach and neat hips that belied the words. 'There's nothing of you, though, is there?'

She made it sound like a fault, and Laurie's slender frame suddenly felt matchstick-thin and totally unattractive.

'My job in recent years hasn't been conducive to putting on weight,' she said with a smile, acquitting

Patsy of malice, for she rather liked the cheerful candour and warm friendliness that made her feel less like a stranger in unfamiliar surroundings.

'Sorting out other people's problems kept you busy, I suppose. I don't know your name, by the way. . . Edward did say, but I've forgotten.'

'Laurie Whittaker. I expect he mentioned that I'm helping out in the practice for a time.'

Patsy's hazel eyes widened abruptly. 'Gosh, I'm so sorry! I thought you were the new housekeeper!'

'An easy mistake to make, apparently,' Laurie said, rather tartly, then relented, smiling at the obviously contrite girl. 'It doesn't matter. You aren't the only one to confuse us.'

The wry allusion went over Patsy's head, naturally. 'Then you're Edward's cousin! I can see the likeness now. I know he's delighted that you were willing to help out at such short notice. We're so busy that you're desperately needed. I man the reception desk at the surgery for a few mornings each week, so we'll be seeing lots of each other.'

She sounded genuinely pleased about that, and Laurie warmed to her unaffected friendliness.

'It's been quite a problem trying to find just the right person to take care of things here—*and* Jamie,' Patsy went on, concerned. 'Housekeepers come and go, mostly unsuitable—and it looks as if the latest hasn't bothered to turn up at all!'

'Yes, I have—and better late than never, by the sound of things.'

The owner of the cool, amused voice was tall and slender and much too elegant for the post she claimed, Laurie thought drily. Judd Harris wouldn't have mistaken *her* for a housekeeper if she'd turned up at Umber House as the new doctor for the practice! In her silk suit and high-heeled court shoes, expensive leather bag slung from a narrow shoulder and shining, ash-blonde hair swept into a stylish knot, the newcomer looked as if she regularly shopped at Harrods.

She smiled from one to the other of the wide-eyed girls. 'Sorry to be so late, but I had trouble with my car. I hope it was all right to walk in unannounced? The door was open and nobody answered the bell. . .'

'It doesn't work,' Jamie volunteered from the garden door, accepting the presence of yet another stranger without surprise.

'I expect it needs new batteries. You must be Jamie. How do you do?' The woman extended a beautifully manicured hand and the little boy shook it gravely. 'Would you like to help to carry in some of my things? Jenefer's unloading the car, but it really needs a man.'

'Sure.' The small chest visibly expanded.

Laurie and Patsy exchanged speaking glances, both recognising a talent for twisting any male, young or old, around a little finger. Laurie wondered drily which of the two men had chosen to employ this attractive, elegant siren as housekeeper to a trio of busy doctors. It seemed unlikely that he'd bothered to check her domestic qualifications for the job!

Jamie dashed off, full of self-importance, and the newcomer looked from one wary girl to the other, smiling. 'I believe one of you must be Dr Whittaker. . .?'

'Me,' Laurie said ungrammatically before further confusion struck yet another blow at her pride.

'I'm Mrs Meridew. I'm a neighbour.' Patsy sounded cool, almost unfriendly. She scrambled from her stool and strolled to the door. 'Time I took my daughter home, I suppose.'

Flat on her back on the lawn, giggling while Angelo washed her face with an exuberant tongue, the little girl ignored her mother's summons. With a shrug, Patsy walked across to jerk the child to her feet, none too gently, and Laurie suspected that while *she* wasn't seen as likely competition, the newcomer posed a very real threat to any hopes concerning Judd Harris nurtured in that curvaceous breast.

'I hoped to be here to welcome you and make sure that everything was ready for you, Doctor. But you're earlier than expected, surely? Dr Fenton said the tenth. . .'

The cool confidence of tone and words irritated Laurie, quite without reason. 'I told him the ninth,' she said shortly. But *had* she? Suddenly she wasn't quite so sure what she and Edward had agreed over the telephone.

If she had turned up a day too soon, then perhaps she could forgive Judd Harris for mixing her up with the obviously expected housekeeper—and maybe she really *did* look every inch a doctor, after all.

CHAPTER TWO

PATSY returned with a tight grip on her small daughter's hand in time to hear the exchange. 'Edward tends to get things mixed up,' she said cheerfully. 'Particularly dates. Say hello, Kay. That's Dr Whittaker, and this is. . .?'

'Mrs Lipski. Serene Lipski.'

Laurie felt that she'd never met anyone whose name matched her personality so well. The woman was cool and calm and totally unruffled, serenely sure of herself in any situation, she suspected. Feeling rather like a gauche schoolgirl by comparison, wishing she'd worn less casual clothes for travelling, she clutched at her ebbing confidence as Edward appeared at the door.

'It looks as if you've brought everything but the kitchen sink, Serene—and that may yet come to light, I imagine!' On the light words, he put an embracing arm about the new housekeeper and smiled into her almond eyes as if they were the only occupants of the crowded room.

Laurie hastily revised her first impressions, realising that they were close friends—and, as Patsy visibly brightened, she was convinced that Judd Harris *was* the main attraction in that direction.

'I seem to have crammed most things into the car,' Serene agreed, laughing up at Edward. 'It's impossible to travel light when one has children and all their toys and trifles. Is Jamie helping Jenefer to unload?'

'Struggling bravely with boxes twice his size. He's a good little lad. He won't be any trouble, and he'll probably be glad of a more settled regime. We badly need someone like you to create order out of our usual chaos. . .*Laurie*!' Belatedly realising his cousin's quiet presence, Edward swept across the kitchen to enfold her in a warm, welcoming embrace. 'Did I know you were coming today?'

'Apparently not,' she said drily. But, warmed by the genuine affection in his hug, she relented and smiled up at him. 'Someone mixed up the dates.'

'Probably me,' he conceded easily. 'How well you look! Did you arrive in time to meet Judd? I must say we can do with you at the surgery these days. We're rushed off our feet.' He turned to the pretty neighbour who regarded them indulgently. 'Any tea in that pot, Patsy? I'm parched!' Swooping on Kay, he swung her up to plant a kiss on her mischievous face. 'Hello, poppet! You look more like your mummy every day,' he told her warmly.

'Was Marcus still asleep?'

As Serene adroitly reclaimed his attention, he set the child down and turned to her with his beaming smile. 'I didn't see him. Would he be in the boot with all those boxes, by any chance?'

She laughed. 'Of course not! He's in his carry-cot on the back seat—or he was when we arrived. Jenefer may have taken him out, of course. He probably needs a nappy change.'

Laurie took care not to meet Patsy's speaking eyes beneath exaggeratedly raised brows as the girl spooned sugar into the tea she had poured for Edward, but she shared her obvious bewilderment. It seemed that the Lipskis had descended en masse! Edward and his partner must be desperate for live-in domestic help to employ an obviously unsuitable woman with two young children—or was it simply that Edward had wanted to help a friend? And himself at the same time, perhaps?

Patsy endeavoured to detach her clinging daughter from Edward's long legs and Angelo bounded in and out, barking wildly, excited by the noise and bustle. Voices were sharply raised out in the echoing, stone-floored corridor as Jamie insisted that he could carry something that an older child declared to be too heavy for him.

There was the sound of a scuffle and a baby began to cry, the piteous wail of a very young infant. Then the two children almost fell into the room, struggling with a carry-cot between them, still squabbling.

Leaping to the rescue, Edward hoisted the carry-cot to the table and bent over the baby with soothing murmurs and kind hands, releasing him from the restraining straps. Then, lifting him out, he cradled him, crooning comfort, while Serene Lipski shushed her young daughter's complaints and Jamie's defensive arguments.

Laurie studied the unexpected tableau with an ironic expression. She had come to Umber for the peace and tranquillity she hoped would soothe past pain and quieten the turmoil of heart and mind and body—and Edward had promised that she would find it in his country practice.

He'd told her that he was temporarily sharing a house with his partner, but had failed to mention Jamie or the expected advent of a new housekeeper and two more children. No doubt the house was large enough to accommodate them all, but it seemed to her at that moment that they would probably be falling over each other's feet for much of the time.

She liked children—but three of them under one roof! Not to mention an excitable and obviously untrained dog whose thrashing tail swept Edward's untouched mug of tea from table to floor with a crash that sprayed Laurie's light skirt and summer sandals with its contents. She jumped to her feet in dismay, hoping that Serene Lipski was as coolly capable of controlling them all as she looked!

'*Out*, Angelo!' Edward's sudden bark was as startling as the dog's shrill voice, and, as the baby wailed anew, his mother moved to take him into her own arms. 'Sorry about that, Laurie,' he said contritely. 'Will it stain?' He turned to Patsy. 'Be an angel and take the kids for an hour while we feed Marcus and get the girls settled.' He swung back to Laurie. 'Did you say you'd seen Judd? Did he explain the sleeping arrangements?'

'Yes—and I've unpacked most of my things. The Blue Room. . .that *is* right, isn't it?' she added, seeing the discomfiture in his expression.

'Well, no, actually.' He seemed ill at ease. 'You see, we thought Serene. . .'

'The bathroom,' Laurie said in sudden, wry understanding.

'And there's the connecting door to the next room that will do nicely for Jenefer.' His smile was apologetic.

'Yes, of course. It's all right, Edward. Just tell me which is my room and I'll move my things.' She stifled her annoyance, but they *were* off to a bad start!

'I know it sounds ghastly, but the attic rooms are really rather nice, and there's a splendid view of the river. . .'

'It sounds perfect.' As Laurie stalked from the room, she thought bitterly that if Judd Harris were around she'd be tempted to kick him from one end of the long garden to the other for thrusting her into such an embarrassing situation.

It wasn't in Laurie's nature to be cross with anyone for long, least of all her kindly cousin, and, besides, she benefited considerably from the change. The attic rooms were, as Edward said, really very nice—low-ceilinged and quaintly angled but with lovely views from the tiny windows, a bedroom with a huge double bed, a smaller room furnished as a sitting-room complete with TV and a bathroom plus a kitchen of her own, small but serviceable.

She hurtled clothes back into cases and scooped up books and photos and toilet articles for transfer, while Mrs Lipski heated milk for Marcus and Edward conveyed various items of her luggage to the Blue Room.

'I do apologise for the mix-up,' he said anxiously,

encountering Laurie on the stairs. 'I don't know why Judd directed you to the wrong room. It was always agreed that you should have the attic flat. I knew you'd like the privacy.'

She didn't bother to explain that his partner had confused her with the new housekeeper. She smiled, and hugged him. 'Don't worry about it, Edward. I'm not complaining.'

He looked relieved. 'I do want you to be happy here, Laurie,' he said earnestly, knowing her recent heartache. 'The housekeeper usually has your rooms, but Serene has a slight heart problem and I don't want her climbing all those stairs a dozen times a day.'

'Is she a patient, Edward?'

'Heavens, no! That would never work! I was at med school with her husband—Paul Lipski, a brilliant man and a very good friend. Surely you've heard me speak of him?'

Laurie couldn't remember. 'Then you and Mrs Lipski go back a long way?' She didn't want to probe, but it would help to know the exact nature of their relationship, she felt.

She was puzzled by the mystery of the missing spouses. For instance, where was Mrs Judd Harris? And why was Serene Lipski apparently moving in without her husband?

'I knew Serene before she and Paul were married—I introduced them, in fact. Sadly, Paul died in a motorway accident just after Marcus was born.' Edward's tone was sombre.

Laurie felt a rush of sympathy. 'Oh, that's terrible!' she exclaimed.

'Tragic. Particlarly as the baby came early and was in Intensive Care at the time. Paul was on his way to the hospital when a lorry ploughed into the back of his car. It's been a difficult time for Serene, naturally. But she's had me to lean on to some extent. I've done what I can, naturally. By the way, as Marcus is a prem he's going to need some extra care over the next few months. As paediatrics is your special province, can I rely on you to keep an eye on him?'

'Yes, of course.' Her trained eye had recognised the baby's prematurity at a glance, and she knew the problems that could arise as well as a mother's very natural rejection of any suggestion that something might be seriously wrong with her delicate infant.

The obvious frailty of Serene Lipski's baby had stirred all Laurie's maternal as well as medical instincts, and she longed to cuddle him close and breathe in his sweet baby smell. Her love for children had taken her into paediatrics, and now it seemed that her qualifications might be needed both in and out of the practice.

'Serene is a very brave lady,' Edward continued. 'She's been struggling to keep the house going and pay Jenefer's school bills and settle the debts that she didn't know existed until she lost Paul. It seemed stupid to let her go on struggling when she could come here and keep house for us. And you now, of course,' he added lightly.

'Well, I've finished moving out.' Laurie indicated

the assortment of articles in her arms. 'All I have to do now is find new homes for this lot. . .' She cocked a listening ear. 'I think that's Mrs Lipski calling you, Edward.'

'*Serene*,' he amended firmly. 'Much more friendly, and she'll be upset if you insist on calling her Mrs Lipski. She's a very warm and caring person, and I know you're going to get on.'

Escaping from the fulsome but possibly valid praise of a woman she had disliked on sight, Laurie hurried away with a vague word and a smile. She sensed something cold and calculating behind the bright smile of someone who looked as if she'd never had to count the pennies in her life!

She couldn't help wondering if the woman was taking advantage of Edward's kind heart, but it was none of her business, and she chided herself for being so uncharitable about a woman who had been widowed in tragic circumstances on top of concern about a new baby. If she stood in Serene Lipski's shoes, no doubt she would be leaning heavily on someone like Edward too!

Some time later, her dark hair damp and curling on her shoulders from a leisurely and very welcome shower, Laurie wondered what was happening about dinner. She was hungry, but no one could expect the new housekeeper to serve up a splendid repast within a few hours of her arrival without assistance. So perhaps she ought to offer to help. Just this once.

Hoping to explore her new surroundings some time that evening, she donned a favourite dress, scoop-necked and sleeveless to show off the becoming tan she had acquired in the few hot days between leaving Hartlake and driving down to Sussex. She had spent those days with her family in Norfolk, lazing and luxuriating in the sun.

To match the bold scarlet flowers that cascaded over the white silk, she added a splash of scarlet beads, an inexpensive but eye-catching trifle, and scarlet, high-heeled sandals. A dash of bright lipstick and a spray of perfume and she felt ready for anything the evening might offer, she decided as she surveyed her reflection in the long mirror.

The slender, pretty girl who looked back at her seemed too young and carefree to be a twenty-six-year-old paediatrician with a badly bruised heart. No wonder few people—and Cris in particular—took her seriously when she wasn't wearing a white coat and wielding a stethoscope!

She could hear Marcus crying with that oddly penetrating wail as she descended the stairs, but there was no sight or sound of the other children or the dog. Laurie marvelled at the good nature of the neighbour who was presumably keeping them all fed and happy for so long.

She was a little puzzled by a strange feeling that she might need such a good friend in the days to come, and she wondered if she had relied too heavily on the thought of Edward's support and felt let down—and maybe even a little jealous—because he seemed so caught up in Serene Lipski's concerns.

It was just like him to sweep any number of lame dogs under his wing, she thought fondly. Including a temporarily homeless partner with a small son, apparently. Edward's concern for people and their problems made him an excellent doctor, and she was really glad of the opportunity to work with him.

She wasn't so sure about Judd Harris.

Laurie paused on the stairs as the GP strode into the hall, tossing his coat and case on a chair. Looking down at him, she observed the height and breadth of the man and the charismatic good looks with detachment. Cris possessed her heart and possibly always would, but she could still admit the elemental magnetism that other women must find attractive.

It was an entirely clinical assessment of the man's physical attractions, of course. She was no longer so surprised that her cousin's practice was apparently inundated by demanding patients. No doubt women in particular flocked to consult Judd Harris on a host of minor problems, Laurie thought drily. Some of them probably fell in love with him too, an occupational hazard for good-looking physicians.

Idly she wondered if he was ever tempted by forbidden fruit. That mouth was strongly sensual. . .

He strolled to the foot of the stairs to look up at her with a frown as Marcus wailed again, even more piteously. 'Shouldn't you be doing something about that infant? It sounds as if he's wet or hungry or both!'

The brusque words coincided with a sudden silence as someone presumably attended to the unhappy baby. 'There doesn't seem to be the need for me to do anything after all, does there?' Laurie riposted sweetly.

She resented his arrogant manner and the continued conviction that she was merely a housekeeper and the mother of the crying child, but she wasn't inclined to put him right. Let him find out the hard way—and be forced to apologise! She imagined that eating humble pie wouldn't come easily to someone like Judd Harris.

He studied her critically. 'On your way out?'

'On my way to the kitchen. I didn't have time to stock the freezer as per instructions, but there has to be *something* to eat in this house,' she said tartly.

He arced a sardonic eyebrow. 'At the risk of seeming to criticise your taste in clothes, may I point out that you don't seem to be suitably attired to prepare dinner for three hungry males?'

'Probably because I haven't the slightest intention of doing so. At the risk of shattering an obviously cherished illusion, may I point out that cordon bleu cookery wasn't part of my training? Perhaps things were different in your day, Dr Harris.' Her tone was deceptively sweet.

The remarkable eyes narrowed abruptly. Then he laughed. 'Dr Whittaker, I presume?' The amused drawl echoed her light-hearted overture at first meeting and mocked his own too-hasty conclusions. 'I thought you were a man.'

Laurie blinked. 'Did you?' She was taken aback by the soft, unrepentant chuckle and the comprehensive, complimentary glance that scanned her from head to toe as if he was seeing her in a totally new light. She froze at the hint of unwelcome interest. 'Edward must have been more than usually vague!'

She swept down the remaining steps with as much

dignity as she could muster in the face of that demoralising survey, only to realise her mistake as he stood his ground and she found herself much too close to him, dwarfed by his powerful frame.

'Edward seldom mentions his family, and I guess I wasn't listening very carefully when he suggested inviting a cousin to help out with the practice. My head was probably full of a patient's problems at the time. And your name isn't particularly feminine, is it? I expected a Laurence. But you're unmistakably a Laura.'

The smile that accompanied the light words would probably have devastated a lesser woman. Even Laurie's pulses quickened fractionally in reponse to its charm. Muscles rippled in the strong shoulders and broad chest as he ran a smoothing hand over the blazing thatch of thick, springy hair in a careless gesture. Rather splendid hands, she noted. Rather a splendid man. She might have found him irresistibly attractive if it wasn't for the way she still felt about Cris. . .

'I owe you an apology,' he said with his slow, warm smile. 'I mistook you for Mrs Lipski, I must admit. But aren't you a day early?'

She sighed. 'I think I must be. But I really thought we'd agreed on the ninth.'

'Vagueness seems to run in the family.' He shook his handsome head in mock reproach. 'I don't know that the practice can stand another absent-minded GP.'

About to bridle, Laurie glimpsed the lurk of

laughter in the glinting eyes, but she wasn't ready to relent and like him. . .not just yet. Maybe never.

'Particularly when she's a woman, perhaps?' she countered acidly.

'Oh, I think I can be persuaded to make allowances for your gender, in the circumstances.' A flicker of warm approval crossed his lean, bronzed face as he smiled down at her.

He didn't seem to be admiring the profusion of silken curls that tumbled about her sun-kissed face or the swell of bronzed breasts above the provocatively low neckline of her suddenly unsuitable dress, but Laurie was abruptly, acutely conscious of her femininity and his raunchy masculinity. She backed instinctively from that overwhelming maleness and her own startling reaction to it.

'Don't patronise me, Dr Harris,' she warned sharply. 'I assure you that it won't be necessary to make allowances for me in or out of the practice!'

Marcus had begun to cry again, and Edward appeared at the head of the staircase with the baby in his arms. 'I thought I heard your voice, Judd. . .'

His partner glanced up with a wry smile. 'I'm surprised you heard anything at all, considering the competition!'

Edward grinned. 'Poor little devil doesn't seem to like his new home, does he? Is there any news of George Fowler?'

'Admitted this afternoon. He's undergoing emergency surgery on a perforated bowel at this very moment. Your diagnosis was right on the ball.' Judd mounted the stairs two at a time, with a long, lithe stride. Whisking Marcus from his partner's arms, he slung him across his own broad shoulder with a paternal as well as a professional expertise. 'What's really the matter with this little lad? Colic?'

'Unsettled after the journey, I imagine. Serene's car broke down on the motorway and she had to wait some time for assistance, although she stressed that she had young children in the car. Not a pleasant experience for her, so soon after losing Paul.'

'Most unfortunate,' Judd agreed. 'How is she?'

'The poor girl has a migraine, and I've given her some pills and sent her to bed. Patsy came to the rescue and took Jamie and Jenefer to her house when it became obvious that Serene wasn't up to taking over the domestic reins right away. I said we'd take care of Marcus between us.' Edward leaned over the ornately carved balustrade to smile at his listening cousin. 'Laurie, do you think you could rustle up some food?'

This was *not* the lifestyle she had envisaged when she agreed to join the practice, Laurie fumed as she made her way to the kitchen. The men might not mind acting as nursemaid to Serene Lipski's baby, but she certainly objected to being maid of all work while the new housekeeper took to her bed!

She felt she could almost enjoy a migraine herself as she cast a smouldering glance at the near-empty freezer and wondered how supplies had been allowed to get so low and what on earth there was in the house for them all to eat.

Moments later, Edward put a reassuring arm about her shoulders. 'Don't worry, Laurie. Serene doesn't want anything and I'll have a pizza sent up from the village. Judd's taking you out for a meal.'

CHAPTER THREE

LAURIE cast a dark glance at the man behind the wheel as the car sped along unfamiliar roads. She had protested, but no one had listened, and she had decided that she was hungry enough to put up with a stranger's company for an hour or two.

She knew absolutely nothing about her cousin's partner except that he had a way with very small children. Marcus had instantly begun to gurgle against that strong, comforting shoulder, she recalled.

The proud profile betrayed nothing of his thoughts as he drove, intent on the narrow ribbon of country lane, his well-shaped hands expert in controlling the big car. Beautiful hands, Laurie observed once more. The hands of an artist or a musician. Or a surgeon, perhaps. She wondered why he had opted for general practice, rewarding but dead-end, and if life in a small country town had proved too boring for Jamie's mother.

'What happened to *Mrs* Harris?' Laurie heard the too-direct and abominably impertinent question zooming about their heads in horror. The words had been searing her brain, but she had had no intention of uttering them. For it was none of her business and she wasn't even particularly interested. Just idly curious.

He shot her a glance. 'She didn't like being married to a GP.'

'Oh. . .' She felt uncomfortable, although there had been no hint of rebuke in his relaxed tone. 'I didn't mean to pry,' she said carefully.

A smile tugged at the warm mouth. 'I guess Edward told you as little about me as he told me about you. And you didn't ask questions any more than I did.'

'Well. . .no.' *She'd* had a lot on her mind, Laurie thought defensively. The break with Cris, the change of job and the rush to find someone to take over her flat for six months. But his lack of interest was surely odd in view of the fact that they would not only be working together in the practice but also sharing a roof. He must have been totally indifferent to her impending arrival or he would have learned that she was a woman long before she set foot in Umber.

'And now you're wondering why Jamie lives with me and not his mother. Women always want to know these things.'

Laurie stiffened at the sardonic tone and the way Judd lumped her with unknown women who apparently clamoured to know all about the attractive physician. It was tantamount to suggesting that her interest in him went beyond the professional!

'There's no need to explain anything to me,' she said crisply. 'Your personal life is entirely your own concern, Dr Harris.'

He smiled. 'It's a rare woman who thinks so, in my experience. However, it's no secret. Jamie's mother went to Australia with the new man in her life, and I wouldn't allow my son to live on the other side of the world from me.'

He sounded so inflexible that Laurie frowned. 'So Jamie is entirely cut off from his mother.'

He shrugged. 'Her choice.'

'Poor little boy!' It was an impulsive exclamation, for she knew the importance of the mother-child bond and the traumas that could result from an abrupt severance at an early age.

Judd's expression hardened. 'He's happy enough. He doesn't even remember his mother.' His tone was brusque.

Laurie thought that was even worse, but she didn't say so, sensitive to his displeasure.

'I'm sorry. I wasn't implying. . .'

'I think you were.' He cut across the murmur of her voice. 'A snap diagnosis without knowing the case history? Is that what they teach at Hartlake these days?'

Laurie flushed. *Arrogant*, *offensive*, *brutal*—but perfectly justified in his resentment of her unthinking words, she admitted wryly, turning her head to gaze at the passing scenery.

She looked so chastened that Judd had to repent. He reached to press the slim fingers that clutched the scarlet leather bag in her lap and smiled into the startled eyes that she turned to him at his touch.

'I didn't mean to be hard on you. But I love the boy. I do what I can to ensure that he doesn't miss his mother, and I suppose I'm sensitive to comment on the way I've mishandled things.'

'Particularly from someone who doesn't know any

of the circumstances and has absolutely no right to comment in any case,' Laurie suggested wryly, surprised and touched by the generous words and gesture.

As Judd returned his hand to the steering-wheel, she found herself missing the brief physical contact and the enveloping warmth of his smile.

'Marla didn't want Jamie,' he went on steadily. 'She's a model—quite a successful one—and she liked being a mother even less than she liked being a doctor's wife. It wasn't her scene.' The bitter words seemed forced out of him as he swung the car into the forecourt of a timbered inn that had been converted to a carvery. 'Now that you know most of the sordid details, perhaps we can leave the past where it belongs for the rest of the evening.'

The note of finality in the deep voice implied that he was weary of the subject of his failed marriage, but the grim set to the mobile mouth told Laurie that he was still hurting, still in love with his ex-wife. She sympathised. For didn't *she* still want Cris, in spite of everything?

Judd steered her across the gravelled courtyard with a hand at her elbow, a careless courtesy that ought not to have conveyed so forcibly the tension in his tall frame.

Laurie felt a chill course the length of her spine as she sensed the deep, implacable anger that burned in him and wondered if that anger consumed him even more fiercely than his love for the absent

Marla. It might even keep him from forgiving and forgetting and finding happiness with someone else.

She imagined there had been affairs. Few women would let such a magnificent prize slip away if he showed even a transitory interest, she felt. Even Laurie admitted to a little buzz of excitement at his touch, although she was disconcertingly aware that her femininity had little impact on him. In fact, his attitude seemed to imply that he had no time for any woman except as an occasional release when a compelling sexuality overcame the reluctance to get involved that was the legacy of a disastrous marriage.

They found plenty of common ground for conversation over a pre-dinner drink. Having qualified at a London hospital, he knew Hartlake and some of its better-known consultants as well as having a few friends among the staff. Medicine was a fellowship of like-minded people, and she learned that they shared many views on patient care in the community.

Laurie was warming to him rapidly when he suddenly ruined their growing rapport by leaning towards her, one arm slung carelessly over the back of the velvet-covered sofa they shared, and saying without any preliminary, 'I gather from Edward that you expected to marry a Hartlake man until recently.'

The direct introduction of a tender subject touched her on the raw, but she knew she had invited it with her own curiosity. 'I wish he hadn't said anything. . .!'

It was involuntary protest that pushed away a stranger's unwelcome concern. But it had obviously been a foolish hope that Edward wouldn't mention her abortive affair with Cris, and Laurie regretted that she had been so effusive about the hopes and dreams that had come to nothing.

'Oh, I'm not sympathising,' Judd told her bluntly. 'Better to find out now that you aren't suited than suffer the misery of trying to make a bad marriage work. But you don't seem the kind to run away, Laurie.'

'I'm not. . .and I haven't!' Indignation swamped the flurry of her senses at the soft sound of her name on his lips.

'Then what brings you to this part of the world? Edward says you stood a good chance of getting a consultancy at Hartlake.'

'Edward exaggerates,' she said crisply. 'Far too much competition.'

'So. . .?' His smile was encouraging.

Laurie shrugged. 'I've been thinking about a change of direction for some time, and I agree with Edward that every group practice should include an experienced paediatric physician. When he suggested that I might like to give it a chance, it seemed an excellent opportunity to find out if I like general practice enough to commit myself to it permanently.'

'A kind of trial marriage,' he drawled. 'Sounds like a good idea. . .'

She glanced at him with suspicion, but his bland expression gave nothing away and the head waiter beckoned to them at that point to indicate that he had a table for them.

The meal was excellent, and Laurie enjoyed every mouthful of the delicious steak and side salad. Judd had ordered claret with the air of a man who knew how to entertain a lady even if her company *had* been thrust on him unawares.

She sipped the delicious wine and listened with half an ear while Judd talked about the practice and some of his more interesting patients. Rather than concentrate on the warmth of his eyes and his lean, handsome face, she admired the swooping elegance of the swans on the river that dreamed past their window table.

It was a glorious evening in high summer and the entire population of Umber seemed to be busy with boats or fishing lines or simply strolling the towpaths as the sun dawdled on its way to bed. The sounds of summer, the food and the wine and the hypnotic timbre of Judd's deep voice combined to lull the tired Laurie into a drowsy sense of well-being.

She knew she ought to be giving her full attention to him, for he was relating many of the details that Edward had failed to mention and she had been too wound up over Cris to ask. But, looking into his eyes, so piercingly blue, set deep amid a warm crinkle of laughter lines that belied the undoubted pain in his past, she felt mesmerised and the image of Cris seemed to blur and fade.

Near to drowning in the depths of that pure, unfathomable blue, a strange, tingling excitement in her veins that she had never felt before, even in

Cris's experienced embrace, all her senses heightened by the dangerous magnetism of a very attractive man, Laurie tore her gaze from the warmly sensual face and concentrated it on her plate.

She blamed the wine and her weariness for the weakness of wanting his touch, his embrace, his potent passion. She had never felt this way about any man, not even Cris, she marvelled—and she wasn't even sure that she liked Judd Harris! So she mustn't allow him to stir her suddenly wayward senses with his powerful sexuality. . .

'Changed your mind about that gâteau?'

She stared. 'Sorry. . .?'

Judd smiled. 'You've been studying it for five minutes.'

Laurie picked up her fork. 'I was listening. . .' She hoped he couldn't read minds as well as stir unwelcome emotions with those incredible eyes!

'You were remembering. It doesn't help—take my word for it.' He regarded her prettily flushed face with a hint of sympathy in his smile. 'Besides, he isn't worth so much doom and gloom.'

He was only echoing the words of many of her friends and, deep down, Laurie recognised their truth. Nevertheless, she bridled. For no girl liked to admit that she had foolishly given away her heart to a man who had never wanted it, and she still clung, however vainly, to a hope that one day Cris might realise what he had lost.

'How would you know?' she demanded coldly.

'I know he hasn't the intelligence to appreciate a real diamond and hold on to it with both hands.' His smile brightened the softly lit corner in which they sat. 'Don't bother that lovely head about him, Laurie. Look to the future.'

She shrugged off the compliment, not at all sure that she wanted his admiring approval, cross with her usually vague cousin who had obviously gone into lurid detail about her broken romance, making a proud pretence that *she* had changed her mind a complete waste of time.

'Advice to the presumably lovelorn?' Her tone was tart. 'Stick to practising medicine and leave that kind of thing to the agony aunts, Dr Harris!'

Maybe it was only fellow feeling from someone who had tasted the bitter waters of rejection for himself, but she didn't welcome his sympathy or his well-meaning suggestions.

'Judd,' he amended. 'It's absurd to stand on ceremony when we're sharing a roof.'

'Not for long.' Laurie was alarmed by the sudden flutter in the pit of her stomach in response to the glow in his smiling eyes. 'I don't think the arrangement will work.' Her privacy was precious to her. It was even more vital to guard her bruised heart from the assault of this man's charm, she told herself firmly.

'Pity. I thought it would work very well as soon as I set eyes on you,' he said lightly.

Laurie shot him a sceptical glance. '*You* thought I was the housekeeper!'

He chuckled. 'And that rankles, does it? At the time, I was too rushed to care who or what you were, frankly. I just felt that you'd fit in and that I liked you. What more did I need to know?'

He was embarrassingly direct. 'Taking a complete stranger on trust can be a mistake,' she warned stiffly, stifling a flicker of gratification at the warmth of his words. 'I might have been *anyone*—walking in uninvited!'

Amusement gleamed in the blue eyes. 'I can't say that I felt threatened. Perhaps because I'm twice your size.'

Judd approved her reluctant laugh. She had a sense of humour as well as a lovely face and a beautiful body and a warmly feminine appeal, he decided, undeterred by a prickliness that he recognised as a natural sensitivity to any hint of unwelcome male admiration.

Laurie skated from the danger of warming to his charisma and the twinkle in his eyes. 'I shall stay at Umber House for the time being, obviously. Edward expects it, and I don't want to disappoint him. But I mean to look around for a place of my own as soon as possible.'

'In the meantime, we must just all do our best to get along,' he suggested drily.

She shrugged. 'Edward and I have always been very good friends. He won't be a problem.'

'But you think that *I* may be.'

She shied from the challenge of the words. 'I really have no idea, Dr Harris. I scarcely know you,' she reminded him coolly.

He smiled into her wary eyes. 'You'll soon know me very well indeed,' he promised.

'It seems unavoidable,' Laurie agreed acidly. 'Seeing that I was sorting out your dirty shirts and socks within a very short time of meeting you!'

His low laugh softened the irregularity of his features, making him seem younger, more vulnerable, so much like Jamie in that moment that Laurie's instinctive resistance to liking him was abruptly undermined. She fought another stir of unwelcome interest in Judd Harris.

'I did apologise for that,' he reminded her, smiling. 'But I can't promise that it won't happen again, I'm afraid. Housekeepers have a habit of departing at speed, and then we simply have to share the chores until we can find someone else. It isn't easy. Two men and a small boy seem to be too much for most women.'

'Not to mention Angelo,' she suggested tartly, still smarting from a vain attempt to remove tea-stains from a favourite skirt.

'Oh, he's usually number one in the popularity stakes, for some reason. That's why he's so spoiled. No one's had the time to train him properly either. But he's only a puppy. He'll grow out of his impossible manners.' Once more, the devastating twinkle lurked in his dancing eyes. 'I'm sorry I can't say the same for myself,' he murmured.

Laurie laughed, almost reluctantly. 'It can't have been easy for you and Edward, running that big house as well as the practice between you, being let down by a succession of housekeepers,' she sympathised. 'But things should improve now, surely? Mrs Lipski has children of her own, for one thing—

company for Jamie—and she seems to be very good friends with Edward.'

'Which isn't a very satisfactory or workable state of affairs, in my opinion,' Judd returned bluntly. 'Even if she *has* been married to a GP for years and knows all about irregular hours and rushed meals and night calls. It seems to me that it won't be easy to terminate the arrangement if it proves disastrous. I've nothing against Mrs Lipski, but I've never believed in mixing business with pleasure.'

'Then you think. . .' Laurie broke off, finishing lamely, 'They've been friends for years, Edward says.'

'Edward can be manipulated, as I expect you know. But I can't see what she hopes to gain from giving up her home to keep house for three busy doctors.' He shrugged. 'Maybe she's just lonely.'

'If you dislike the arrangement, why don't you move out?' Emboldened by a fractional shift in his attitude, Laurie was curious to know why he remained at Umber House in view of the erratic domestic scene.

Judd looked beyond her questioning eyes to the river and the reddening sky as the sun began to set. 'I don't want to uproot Jamie. He had an unsettled few years until I joined forces with Edward. He hasn't had the time or the attention that he needs, and there's no doubt that he's been bewildered by so many women coming and going in his young life.' He returned his brooding gaze to her intently listening face. 'Too many "mothers"—and not one of them the right one,' he said flatly.

Laurie observed the bitter twist to the mobile mouth and sympathised, but she was slightly shaken by the candid admission that his wife had been succeeded by a number of women. No one could expect an attractive, divorced doctor to lead a celibate life, as long as he was discreet and avoided affairs with his patients. But it seemed that he was as much of a womaniser as Cris, the kind of man that a sensible girl tried not to tangle with however attracted she might be, and that was a pity, for she had been on the verge of liking him.

Judd appraised her as she drank a little of her wine in a tactful silence. She was a very pretty girl with a superb figure and a quick intelligence. It was a long time since he had looked at any woman with more than fleeting and purely sexual interest, but he found himself looking again and again at Laurie Whittaker, so delicately feminine and with a vulnerable appeal that aroused all his protective instincts as well as a strong stir of desire.

Soft, scented curls dancing as she turned her head, sapphire eyes fringed by long, dark lashes and smudged with weariness, a hint of obstinacy in the set of her chin but with the smiling sweetness of a mouth that tempted a man's kiss, there was character as well as charm in the distinctive oval face.

Judd felt she was the kind of girl who would be loving, loyal, strong in her support of any man she eventually married, unlike his errant wife.

His gaze strayed to the slender throat, encircled by the bright beads that betrayed a feminine liking for colourful trifles, and further still to the sun-warmed breasts that tempted a man's caress. He moistened a suddenly dry mouth with his own wine and crushed the rising tide of longing. Life was complicated enough without an unprofessional interest in a colleague to make matters worse, he told himself firmly.

Laurie's heart jolted in alarm as their eyes met. She was used to the reaction that her face and figure apparently engendered in some men, but she wasn't prepared for her own involuntary reponse to the fierce, aching hunger in the way that Judd Harris was looking at her.

Pulses racing, a molten lava of longing hurtling through unwary veins, she stared at his mouth and fantasised the taste and the heat and the urgency of his kiss, the caress of those strong hands on her body and the soaring excitement as he made expert love to her—and then she caught hastily at runaway thoughts and feelings evoked by a stranger whose embrace tempted her so much it was shocking.

'I must have been in the devil of a hurry to think you could be a widow with two children,' Judd said abruptly. 'You look about sixteen. I suggest you pin up that hair and wear a tailored suit when you put in an appearance at the surgery, or the patients might think you're just playing at being a doctor.'

And a respectable GP might just forget himself and shock a roomful of waiting patients by sweeping an irresistibly alluring colleague into his arms, he thought ruefully, alarmed by the fierce battering at the defences he had erected about his emotions on the day that Marla walked out of his life.

CHAPTER FOUR

HIS censorious tone shattered the foolishly fanciful image of him as tender lover as well as the illusion that his gaze held a dangerous admiration.

'I believe you think that too,' Laurie said briskly. 'But I have all the right qualifications, and I can assure you that I do know my job.'

Judd nodded indifferently. 'You can enjoy proving it to me.' He studied her with narrowed eyes that held a critical light. 'I must say I'd have vetoed Edward's suggestion if I'd known you only wanted to come here to nurse a broken heart.'

It was deliberately caustic. In his experience, few women liked plain speaking and even fewer forgave the probing of a wound, and he felt that encouraging Laurie Whittaker to dislike him was probably a sure way to keep her at a safe distance.

He had her emotional security in mind as well as his own. A girl who had been recently disappointed in love was vulnerable and much too ready to believe herself in love again—and he had nothing to offer her but more disappointment.

Laurie glowered. 'You quite mistake the matter,' she told him coldly. 'My heart *isn't* broken, and that *isn't* the case!'

'I suspect it's a part of your reasons for leaving Hartlake, however.' Rather too late, Judd wondered if he should have left Umber, taking Jamie, and endeavoured to make a fresh start somewhere else if not with someone else. But his roots were here and so were Jamie's, and Marla had done enough damage to their lives without allowing painful memories of her to drive them from the district.

'To some extent, perhaps,' Laurie agreed stiffly. 'I needed a change of scene, to meet new people and make new friends. Is that so wrong?'

'Not wrong. Just not the best of motives for joining a busy medical practice, perhaps.'

Her sapphire eyes sparked with indignation. 'Don't worry about it, Dr Harris. My motives, whatever they may be, won't affect my professional judgement or my treatment of your patients.'

'You'll hear about it from me if they do.' Judd meant the grim warning. Over the years, he had worked hard to build up the practice and probably sacrificed more than his marriage to its demands.

He had never allowed his marital problems or anxiety about Jamie to interfere with his whole-hearted commitment to the community, and he knew he would have little patience with a colleague who dissolved in tears or made life-threatening mistakes in diagnosis or prescription whenever someone or something reminded her of her lost love.

His eyes were hard, suddenly so cold that Laurie was chilled. He was difficult, enigmatic, unpredictable. Smiling one moment, scowling the next—and no doubt determined to punish every woman he met for the hurt done to him by his ex-wife!

As they left the riverside restaurant, she glanced

wistfully at the rosy swath of water beneath the rapidly setting sun and wanted to linger beside its still, soothing tranquillity.

Here, in these lovely surroundings, miles from London and Cris, the ache in her breast had already lessened, just as Edward had promised. But Judd swept her towards the car with an inexorable hand in the small of her back that sent another of those strange shivers scuttering down her spine. . .

Believing that the sunshine streaming through the windows and falling across the big bed had woken her, Laurie burrowed deeper into the pillows, reluctant to emerge from a delicious if most unlikely dream about a man she had met for the first time less than twenty-four hours before.

'I've brought your breakfast, Doctor. . .'

The words brought her tumbling from the bed and hurrying to take the tray. Even at that early hour, Serene Lipski looked immaculate in crisp blouse and tailored skirt, not one shining hair out of place and just the right amount of make-up delicately applied, her inconvenient migraine obviously a thing of the past.

Laurie pushed the mass of tangled curls from her face and thought how inviting the tray looked with its pot of steaming coffee, scrambled eggs and bacon, several slices of toast and miniature pot of honey—all apparently conjured out of thin air, for she had found nothing so appetising in fridge or cupboards the previous evening.

'You really mustn't wait on me,' she protested.

'I'm sure that isn't the arrangement, and so many stairs aren't good for you.'

Serene's smile was reassuring. 'Edward told you I have a heart problem, didn't he? It isn't really much of a problem, merely a slight murmur that I've had all my life. I'm quite fit enough to climb a few stairs. He's just being over-protective.'

The faint complacency of her tone jarred on Laurie, but she did her best to warm to the woman for Edward's sake, for she suspected that her cousin was very much in love with his friend's widow.

'There's no need for you to provide me with breakfast, however,' she said firmly. 'I have my own small kitchen and I shall get in some stores today and see to myself each morning. You have more than enough to do, looking after the children.'

Serene looked with wistful envy around the pleasant bedroom and through the open door into the small, cosy if cluttered sitting-room with its bright chintzes and sunny aspect. 'Your rooms are lovely. You should be very comfortable up here, Doctor.'

It was obvious to Laurie that she would have preferred the attic rooms for herself and her children, and she wondered if Edward was putting pressure on the woman to enter into a more intimate relationship than she wished at this stage.

'It is nice,' she agreed lightly. 'But I'm perfectly willing to change with you if you feel these rooms will be better for the children.'

It was a generous gesture, sincerely meant. She might not like Serene Lipski very much, but she did feel sorry for her situation. It couldn't be easy to face the prospect of raising two children on her own or to give up her home to take care of two—no, *three* doctors, someone else's child and a boisterous dog. No doubt it had been her own decision, but she must be feeling a little daunted now that she had actually taken up residence at Umber House.

'That's very kind, but I think we should leave things as they are,' said Serene. 'Jenefer does have her own bedroom, you see—and I can put Marcus in with her as soon as he sleeps through the night. At the moment, he's only disturbing me.'

'I expect you're having a few problems with his eating and sleeping,' Laurie sympathised.

'He isn't ill, you know,' Serene said sharply.

Like many mothers of babies who differed in even the slightest degree from others, she was instantly on the defensive. It was the first crack in that ice-cool composure that Laurie had observed, and she understood its cause. Knowing the hidden anxieties, well experienced in dealing with their causes and feeling that she might be of some help, she was suddenly more at ease with Serene.

'I'm sure he's perfectly healthy, and he's certainly a beautiful baby. He just has some catching up to do, like most babies who come into the world earlier than expected, that's all,' she said lightly. 'I dare say Edward has told you that prems were my speciality at Hartlake? If you have any worries about Marcus at any time that you'd like to talk over with me, please don't hesitate.'

Serene turned to the door with no indication that she appreciated or would take advantage of the well-meant offer. 'Edward asked me to remind you that surgery starts at eight-thirty. He's leaving about ten past, if you'd like to be ready.'

It had been agreed that Laurie should 'sit in' for that first morning to learn the system, get acquainted with the staff and find her way about the newly built health centre. She had meant to be up early, but she had slept long and deep after a day that had seemed jam-packed with event since she had closed the door of her flat in London and set off on a new venture.

Serene didn't quite close the door as she left, and Laurie returned from brushing her teeth to find that Angelo had sneaked in and stolen the bacon from her tray. He sat in the middle of the room, grinning wickedly and quite unashamed, tail thumping in such obvious delight at having found her again that it was impossible not to laugh and forgive him, although it meant forgoing her breakfast. For who knew where that great, lolloping tongue had explored while she was in the bathroom?

A little too late, Jamie hurtled into the room to grab Angelo's collar and scold him so thoroughly even before learning his crime that it was instantly obvious to Laurie that the dog was an incorrigible thief. She began to understand just why so many housekeepers came and went in her cousin's house.

'I thought his taste ran to bread and jam,' she said ruefully, returning the ravaged tray to the kitchen to find that Jamie had been before her with the tale of his pet's depravity.

She shook her head to the concerned offer of a freshly cooked meal and brushed off Edward's contrite apology with the wry admission that she was to blame for not noticing that the bedroom door was ajar.

Judd glanced up from the newspaper he was idly scanning. 'It makes sense to keep doors firmly secured in this establishment, you'll find,' he declared drily. 'If it isn't dogs, then it's kids.'

'I only put Marcus down on your bed for a moment,' Jenefer murmured defensively as she carefully poured fresh coffee into his cup.

'With a wet nappy. On my clean shirt.'

But he put an arm about the little girl and hugged her to show he didn't bear a grudge, and Laurie realised that he wasn't really cross, just resigned. Few men would have failed to be angry in similar circumstances, she felt, warming to him.

She glanced from one to the other in the bright, sun-dappled kitchen. The eight-year-old Jenefer seemed a practical and cheerful child, with her long golden plaits and dimpled smile. She had taken to her new surroundings like a duck to water and already seemed at ease with both Edward and Judd. She had taken Jamie firmly in hand too, although it was doubtful that such a well-behaved little boy needed her supervision and instruction.

With her smiling efficiency and capable air, Serene seemed to have slotted into her new role as if it had been tailor-made for her, and she obviously meant to make herself indispensable to everyone's comfort. A beaming Edward seemed well satisfied with the success of his schemes, and no doubt his partner was thankful that things were likely to run more smoothly in the future, both at home and in the practice.

Laurie felt she was the only one who would never fit comfortably into this rather eccentric household.

There was a sudden bustle of activity as an anxious Jamie hurtled into the kitchen, shouting that he'd lost his school bag, Jenefer was sent to bring down the baby for his feed, and Edward suddenly realised that it was time to leave for morning surgery.

A leather bag swinging from her shoulder and her medical bag in her other hand, Laurie encountered Judd as she ran down the stairs. He emerged from Jamie's room with the missing satchel and quickened his pace to catch up with her.

'Ready for the fray?' Looking over the banister rail at Jamie, waiting anxiously in the hall, he lifted the satchel high above his head in triumph.

'Yes, I think so.'

'You look. . .' He hesitated, as if he sought just the right word but actually wondering how she would react if he voiced the compliment which had flown to mind.

'*Older*?' Laurie suggested crisply, sure that his sweeping glance mocked the knot of thick curls drawn into a huge butterfly slide on the nape of her neck, not quite heeding his advice to put up her hair but endeavouring to look slightly more mature for the benefit of the patients she would meet that morning.

Perhaps foolishly, she was also slightly sensitive about the classic grey suit and pale grey silk shirt and good string of pearls she was wearing in a conscious effort to rival Serene Lipski's effortless elegance.

'The part,' Judd amended smoothly, with a crinkle of amusement.

'Maybe that's the intention.' Flustered by the unexpected flutter of her pulses as she met his laughing eyes, Laurie impulsively crouched beside Jamie to straighten the carelessly knotted tie and smooth the burnished tousle of his hair. 'There, that's better, isn't it?' She smiled warmly at the little boy, who had endured her ministrations with a polite placidity.

'Thank you, Dr Whittaker,' Judd prompted with a press of his hand on his son's shoulder.

'Oh, that's too much of a mouthful,' Laurie protested. '*Laurie* will do.'

From the doorway, she watched them walk to Judd's car and thought how alike father and son were, even to the swing of shoulders and the lope of long stride and the tilt of handsome, bronzed heads.

Jamie was a dear little boy. How *could* his mother have walked away from him, gone to the other side of the world without him? And Judd, so attractive, so obviously caring and considerate—how *could* the unknown Marla have left him for another man?

Unexpectedly, her heart swelled with compassion for the man and his child, both abandoned by a woman who should have been the centre of their universe.

'I really had no idea that Umber was this size!' she

exclaimed as Edward drove her through busy streets towards the heart of the town. 'I expected a village!'

'It was originally two sleepy villages, Great and Little Umber, but since the motorway was extended to the nearby coastal town it's become a popular dormitory suburb, I'm almost sorry to say. We've had a terrific building boom in the past year or two—new estates, shops and schools and even a business park. Now we've a steadily growing population and not enough doctors to take care of it.'

'So that's why the health centre was so necessary.'

Edward nodded, slowing down for a lollipop lady who ushered a stream of small children across the busy road to a newly built primary school. 'We badly need your help with the influx of new patients, particularly the children, and I hope you're going to like general practice and decide to stay at the end of your six months.'

Laurie felt it was much too soon to commit herself to anything. 'I like what I've seen so far,' she temporised.

'Does that include Judd?' he asked slyly.

'It even includes Angelo,' she evaded lightly.

Edward grinned. 'Very magnanimous, in the circumstances.'

The modern health centre had replaced the antiquated surgery in a crumbling Victorian villa where Judd's father and grandfather before him had treated their patients. Edward hoped that present-day patients would welcome Laurie's warmth of heart and sincere feel for her work, and he was sure her youthful looks would put younger patients instantly at their ease

For some time, he had argued that the practice needed a paediatrician, and a kindly fate had come up with the perfect solution, in his view. Edward wanted his cousin to be a permanent member of the practice, but he needed Judd's firm support for the idea.

His partner's chilly reserve and defensive antagonism towards most women was the result of Marla's desertion and a bitter divorce, but it would melt before the warmth of Laurie's sympathetic personality, he decided with incurable optimism.

As she accompanied her cousin into the health centre, Laurie had the new-girl feeling that she recalled from school and university and medical student days at Hartlake.

Patsy was on duty that morning, greeting newly arrived patients, making appointments, handing out repeat prescriptions and referral letters, answering the constantly buzzing switchboard and managing to stay cheerful and unruffled as well as miraculously remembering names and conditions.

She smiled a welcome. 'You're keen to start work, aren't you?' she teased with her easy friendliness. 'I thought you'd take a few days to settle in and get used to us!'

'It rather looks as if I'm needed here, doesn't it?' Laurie indicated the rapidly filling reception area and the queue of patients at the desk.

Edward ushered her into the large, open-plan office where the medical secretaries dealt with patient records and huge amounts of correspondence as well as the complex accounting demanded of every practice.

'Judith—and Lesley.' He identified the bright-faced girls who ensured the smooth running of practice affairs behind the scenes and they smiled a welcome before bending busy heads over their work.

The practice sister was a middle-aged professional in navy dress and traditional cap who obviously stood no nonsense from patient or doctor. Sister Beavis was a force to be reckoned with, Laurie recognised with a mix of admiration and amusement. Just the kind of nurse that any doctor would want at his or her side in a crisis, however.

Most of Edward's patients that morning were small children with runny noses or upset tums or noisy chests or easily diagnosed rashes, minor complaints that still required a doctor's diagnosis and advice. Laurie quickly realised how much of such routine work she could lift from her cousin's burdened shoulders, and long before the end of surgery she was installed in a consulting-room of her own and seeing those children who might otherwise have had a long wait for attention.

The measles epidemic was on the wane, but viral meningitis had lately become a cause for concern throughout the country. Having dealt with two serious cases just before leaving Hartlake, Laurie felt qualified as well as concerned to detect incipient signs of the disease in a child's ear infection.

She went to consult with Edward and walked slap into Judd, newly arrived at the surgery after a round of house visits. 'Oh, Judd! I wonder if you can advise me. . .' she began.

He paused. 'Got a problem?'

She hesitated briefly. 'I think I've a case of early meningitis.' Absurdly, all her confidence seemed to ebb before the powerful presence of a man whose experience of serious childhood complaints was possibly not as extensive as her own.

Judd frowned. 'Sure about that?' It was instinctive gut reaction to the potential threat to other patients rather than a slur on her competence, but he saw her stiffen and knew she had taken offence. She was as prickly as a hedgehog, he thought impatiently.

'Not without proper tests, of course. But I do know what to look for,' Laurie said tersely, and went on to detail the symptoms and her cogent reasons for believing that the child was incubating the disease.

He listened intently, nodding agreement, putting the occasional question. 'It sounds as if your diagnosis could be right,' he agreed, smile and tone intended to soothe the ruffled feathers of her professional pride. 'It's some time since I came across a case, I must admit. I rather hoped we'd escape the new outbreak. However, let's hope it's viral rather than meningococcal. . .' The latter was much more deadly. Viral meningitis usually responded well to treatment if detected in the early stages. 'How old is the child?'

'Just three,' she repeated. 'He's an only child and doesn't attend nursery school or play group, so it's possible that the infection may be contained.'

Judd gave an approving nod. She'd asked all the right questions. It was important that the source of the infection should be traced, but that was a job for the local health officer who would need to be informed of their suspicions.

'You'd like the boy admitted right away, I take it? Do you want me to arrange it?'

'Please. They won't know my name at the General yet, will they?'

'Oh, we've already told them that you're joining the practice. The consultant in charge of the paediatric unit says he knows you, by the way. A chap called Curtis. Let me have the Baker child's notes and I'll call him right away.'

'Thanks.' Laurie went back to the consulting-room to break the news to the mother that it seemed wise to have Scott admitted to hospital so that his ear infection could be properly monitored. She said nothing about the possibility that the child had contracted meningitis, for she saw no good reason to alarm the mother at this stage.

Difficult to diagnose because its symptoms were so similar to those of other ailments, the disease could lay a child low before mother or GP saw the danger signals. It was only her recent experience of such cases that had alerted Laurie, and she was well aware that she could be mistaken.

She hoped it was so.

CHAPTER FIVE

BY THE end of morning surgery, she had become Dr Laurie to most of her small patients and their mums. Laurie was pleased by the indication that she was already accepted.

Everyone was so friendly and, very different from Hartlake, everyone had time to get to know each other. The health centre was a busy place with a number of clinics that lessened the load on the Northwood General, the local hospital, and its liaison office for the district nurses and midwives and health visitors.

She found herself without transport back to Umber House, for an unthinking Edward had left to keep an appointment and Patsy had shopping to do before she went home. In future, she would have her own car to ferry her about, but for the moment she was dependent on a taxi—or Judd's instant offer of a lift. It seemed churlish to refuse.

As they walked to his car, his tall frame at her side seemed an already familiar presence. It was surprising how much she had seen of him since her arrival only twenty-four hours before, but that was an inevitable spin-off from working together and sharing the same roof.

'I expect you're ready for something to eat.' Judd slid behind the wheel and switched on the ignition in one fluid movement. 'I know an excellent Italian restaurant that you might like to try.'

'I don't usually bother with much more than a sandwich in the middle of the day,' Laurie demurred.

'You didn't eat breakfast, as I recall.'

She smiled ruefully. 'Well, no. . .' Patsy had brought her coffee and biscuits halfway through the busy morning, but that had only staved off her present feeling of emptiness. 'And I do like Italian food,' she weakened. 'But my treat this time—I insist.'

Inevitably, they talked shop—the work of the practice, Sister's invaluable experience that outweighed her doughty manner, various patients that Laurie had met that morning, as well as Scott Baker who was already undergoing tests to confirm or disprove her tentative diagnosis.

'I dare say you recall from your GP training that things are very different from treating patients in hospital,' said Judd. 'For instance, once you refer someone for specialist treatment or surgery, he's out of your hands. You'll probably miss the regular contact and the feeling that your fingers are on the pulse of his treatment and progress. I know I do,' he admitted.

'It may not be easy to divorce myself from concern about a patient I've seen in surgery,' Laurie agreed. 'I like to see a case through from beginning to end. That's why I opted for a hospital career.'

He nodded. 'Whereas I've always liked the roundness of practice work. Knowing the background and the medical history helps to treat the particular problem that brings a patient to the surgery each time.'

'Obviously you get to know your patients much better than is possible when they're hospitalised.'

'Yes, indeed. There's a personal involvement in dealing with every member of a family from newest baby to grandparent that's very rewarding, and one only gets that continuity in a small town or country practice. Hospital doctors tend to be too clinical, too detached, simply because they don't have the time to get to know patients as people.' He smiled at her to show that he meant no offence with the blunt words.

'I suppose that's true to some extent. But I'm used to a great deal of involvement with my patients and their families.' She wondered if he knew the effect on her strangely heightened senses of that warm, speaking smile. 'Too much so, at times. . .' She was remembering the dreadful abuse of a baby and how grieved she had been that all her training and dedication had failed to save a life.

A shadow crossed her face and a shudder caught at her slight frame as she thought of the paltry prison sentence that would probably be meted out when the man responsible for that terrible suffering and unnecessary death finally came to trial. Her own brief but memorable encounter with him had convinced Laurie that he was an unfeeling, irresponsible brute, and it was hard for her to subscribe to the currently popular view that such people needed psychiatric help rather than punishment.

The sudden bleakness of beautiful eyes and the betraying quiver of a soft mouth pierced Judd with a sharp, poignant longing to hold her close and kiss away an unmistakable sadness.

'What is it, Laurie?' His tone was gentle. So was the touch of his hand on the restless fingers that tweaked at the folds of the tablecloth.

Laurie looked into his expressive eyes and felt a catch at her heart. He was so much nicer than she had realised, and suddenly, encouraged by his kindly concern, she found herself telling him about the night-long vigil beside a baby's cot in a side-ward of the paediatric ITU at Hartlake as well as the disturbing assault on herself by Keenan's stepfather that she had never mentioned to anyone else, not even Cris.

'You reported it to the police, of course.'

She shook her head and the dark, shoulder-length curls danced about her face. 'No. I couldn't face all the questions or the insistence on prosecution, particularly once I knew he'd been charged with Keenan's murder. I just wanted to forget it had happened. After all, he didn't do me any actual physical harm—it was just the way he looked and the things he said and the way he touched me. . .'

Laurie shuddered again, recalling the ugly look and even uglier words and the trail of nail-bitten fingers across her shocked breast. Judd's strong hand tightened over her own in a comforting clasp, and she pulled herself together.

'My fault for allowing him into the room, I suppose. But I didn't know what he was like or that he was responsible for Keenan's injuries. He said he was the baby's father, and he seemed concerned—and a doctor doesn't expect to be assaulted by an anxious relative in a hospital ward, even if she is a woman and there isn't anyone else around at the time.'

'Not a nice experience,' Judd said quietly.

'I'd always felt that a white coat was all the protection I needed, even when dealing with drunks and hooligans in Casualty.' Her smile was wry. 'But this was a man who thought that any woman on her own was fair game—and he didn't even have the excuse of being drunk.'

'Bastard.' The quiet word was shocking in its intensity.

Seeing the tensing of Judd's jaw, the hardening of his mouth and the keen flash of fury in his eyes, Laurie was sure that Keenan's obnoxious stepfather would have received short shrift at his hands if he'd caught the man molesting her that night.

Judd was the kind of champion that any woman would like to have around, she realised, knowing that if she *had* confided in Cris he would have dismissed the incident as a mere bagatelle and an occupational hazard, insensitive to the effects of such an encounter on someone like herself.

'I can't help feeling that I must have said or done something to give him the wrong impression. Encouraged him somehow to think I wouldn't object. . .' She bit her lip.

'Men like that don't wait for encouragement.' There was biting scorn in Judd's deep voice. 'You must overcome the feeling that any of it was your fault, Laurie. You were just doing your job—and doing it damn well too, I've no doubt. You weren't responsible for that moron's attitudes or his behaviour.'

Laurie smiled at him gratefully. The strongly reassuring words were just what she needed to put the whole business into a comforting perspective.

Judd's answering smile was guarded as he suddenly realised how near he was to the danger of warming to her sweetness and softness and appealing femininity. The danger of caring all over again, of admitting another woman into a heart that had resolved never to love again.

Women took all that a man could give and used it to their advantage and then left when something more attractive came along, he reminded himself grimly. Only a fool ignored the lessons of the past.

For the rest of the meal, it seemed to Laurie that he was rather distant, and she was reminded of the sudden cooling of the previous evening. Perhaps, like herself, he mistrusted any relationship that seemed to border on the personal.

She had been so content, so caught up in the work she loved, until Cris had swept her off her feet. She had stupidly forgotten her sensible resolve to avoid romantic encounters with any of her colleagues and invited heartache and humiliation as well as grapevine gossip with her affair with Cris. Laurie had felt forced into leaving her very good job at Hartlake for a doubtful future as a country GP—and she doubted if Cris had minded or missed her!

First love could be very painful and very disappointing for someone who had left it so late to try it. But perhaps it hadn't cut as deep as she'd supposed. For she was drawn to another man much sooner and more strongly than she would have believed possible when Cris had been the most important person in her life.

Having kept most men carefully at bay throughout the years as medical student, houseman and paediatric registrar, perhaps she had been ripe for making a fool of herself over a surgeon whose affairs were many and meaningless.

Laurie was thankful that she'd refused to surrender her virginity, even if her obstinacy had cost her the happiness that had suddenly seemed within her grasp. She had felt that too many women had fallen unresisting into Crispin Page's arms and that he would respect and admire her all the more if she withheld her favours until she was convinced that he really cared for her.

It hadn't worked out like that. Cris had tired of a pursuit that was getting him nowhere and looked somewhere else for the sexual satisfaction that she denied him.

Knowing him, it had been inevitable, she realised now. But it hurt that he had loved her so little when she had been ready to love him so much. Hopefully, she had salvaged her heart before it was too late. The thought of him with someone else already hurt less than it had.

One day she might feel that she could trust some man to want her for more than just sex. For the moment she was suffering from a bruised if not broken heart and a badly dented pride, and she had no intention of getting involved with any man again for some time to come.

So she could sympathise with the feelings of someone who had even more cause to shy away from emotional entanglement. Who could blame Judd if he found it impossible to settle down permanently with any woman after his first experience of marriage?

Instead of going back to Umber House, she returned to the health centre with Judd and sat in on the weekly conference of local GPs, district nurses and health visitors. Her work in the rapidly growing practice would involve her in a number of home visits and liaison with the social services, and she welcomed the opportunity to meet some of the people with whom she would need to interact in the coming months.

It was interesting to observe Judd as he talked passionately but intelligently about the needs of the community and the amount of extra funds that must be provided by the NHS to meet them.

'We've a fast-expanding population that covers the entire spectrum from an increase in newborns to a growing number of aged, and there simply aren't the doctors or the facilities to cope with all their medical requirements,' he stated bluntly. 'If the NHS can't provide them then we have to look to the private sector, whether or not it goes against one's principles.'

'Grinding your own axe again, are you, Harris?'

Laurie glanced at the speaker, a florid-faced GP whose name she couldn't remember but who seeemed to have little liking for Judd. The feeling was obviously reciprocated, for she saw that Judd was having to hold on to his temper.

'Everyone here knows that I'd like to open a private clinic to take care of the minor surgery that ties up the operating theatres and the valuable time of the surgeons at the Northwood General. I make no secret of it, Randall—and I don't quite understand your opposition. Every GP in this room is qualified to carry out minor ops, including yourself, and your support as well as your assistance in setting up the project would be invaluable.'

'You need my contacts to drum up the finance too, no doubt,' the man said with a sneer.

'Money isn't the immediate problem. I already have a suitable property in mind and the funds arranged to convert it into a clinic and staff it for the first year. I hope to interest the right people to form a trust fund, and that's where your contacts will be useful, I agree.'

'This is turning into a meeting to discuss a private project,' Sister Beavis said calmly. 'May I suggest that we get back to the agenda and Mr Jolley's special needs?'

Her quiet tone brought the meeting back to order and the subject was shelved. But Laurie sensed from the set to Judd's jaw that the project was dear to his heart and would be mentioned again and again until he won the day. She couldn't imagine him *not* getting his way when something was important to him.

As they left the meeting, Judd invited Laurie to accompany him on a visit to Keith Jolley, a paraplegic patient who had been the only survivor of a multiple car crash some months before.

'He's having a fight with the local council over the conversion of his house,' he explained as he manoeuvred his big car through the narrow streets of the older part of the town. 'Keith's father went ahead and built an extension to provide a downstairs bedroom and bathroom before he'd got planning permission. He knew it was risky, but Keith was fretting to be home and his consultant wouldn't discharge him until he had suitable home surroundings.'

'Sounds reasonable,' Laurie agreed.

'It is reasonable, but bureaucracy won't agree. The consultant has done his best and I've written letters and attended meetings, but we're still fighting to keep the extension. There are other problems too—financial as well as social.'

Keith Jolley greeted them with cheerful good humour in spite of his many problems. He was delighted to be out of hospital at last and home with his young wife and two babies, but it seemed unlikely that the arrangement could continue unless he received considerable assistance from the social services.

Annabel Jolley had been a staff nurse at the Northwood General before her marriage, working in the orthopaedics unit, by one of those strange ironies of life, and she had nursed many people with injuries similar to those suffered by her husband.

'Nursing strangers is a very different kettle of fish from nursing the man you love,' she admitted to Laurie as she made tea for the visitors while Judd talked to his patient. 'I don't mind what I have to do for Keith, naturally. But he hates some of the indignities. Says he'd rather have a district nurse come in to see to his stoma than have me do it. But they have so many other people to look after, and I'm on the spot!'

'It must be very hard for you,' Laurie said gently.

Annabel held back tears, just as she had done so bravely ever since the accident. 'Worse for Keith. He was always on the go. Not just the business—he was building up a good reputation as a painter and decorator. It was every sport you could imagine—rugger, squash, golf, tennis, cricket—and he had Simon kicking a ball before he could walk! Training him for the local football team. . .' She laughed shakily.

Laurie was desperately sorry for the young couple whose plans and dreams for the future had been shattered so suddenly. She couldn't even offer the usual assurances that Keith would continue to make progress until he was back on his feet. Judd had made it plain that Keith would never walk again and that it was only a matter of time before already failing kidneys required him to be hospitalised again. She realised that Annabel Jolley was well aware of the situation and doing her best to make light of it and hide the unpalatable facts about the future from her husband. The dispute with the local council was the least of her worries, but it gave Keith something to think about, she added.

'Will you be visiting instead of Dr Harris in future, Doctor?' Annabel asked as she carried the tea-tray through to the rooms that had been hastily added to the house by her builder father-in-law.

'I'm not sure.' Laurie looked at Judd.

'Keith will remain my patient. I merely brought Dr Whittaker along to meet you both. I'm not giving up the best cup of tea in town and the opportunity to discuss the chances of Umber United's getting into the League,' Judd said with a grin. 'Surely you don't think my calls are purely professional?'

It was good to see the cheerful grin that greeted his words and the tears chased from Annabel's eyes, and it was an insight into Judd's attitude to his patients that Laurie appreciated. He had a light touch that didn't detract from his perception of their problems, she suspected—and it was obvious from the little conversation she'd had with Sister Beavis and Patsy earlier in the day that he was much liked.

She could understand why. She liked him, too.

'How are you on obstetrics?' he asked the following evening, entering the sitting-room where she was talking over a day that had been full of interest with her cousin. Judd was on call and had just answered a summons from the telephone.

Laurie looked doubtful. 'I'm used to treating children. I may be a bit rusty when it comes to delivering them!'

He smiled. 'It may not come to that. But that was a call from a Mr Cook. His wife seems to have gone into labour, but the baby isn't due for another two months. It's probably one of the usual false alarms for a primigravida. She's rather older than most to be having her first baby, so there may be some cause for concern. Care to come with me and be introduced to the mother of a possible new patient for your list?'

'Laurie's had a long day,' Edward protested.

'No longer than anyone else, and she needs to learn her way around the town,' Judd said firmly. 'She'll be going out on night calls on her own by next week.'

'I'd love to come.' Laurie smiled at her weary cousin, slumped in a chair with a welcome drink in his hand. 'Put your feet up while you can—the next call might be for you!'

'I'm hoping that's it for tonight,' he told her as Serene came into the room, having finally got a fretful Marcus off to sleep. He got to his feet. 'Is he settled at last? Sit down and have a drink, darling. You look as if you need one!'

Laurie wondered if that endearment with its betraying concern had been unconscious. But there was little doubt in her mind that her cousin was in love with Serene and hoped to replace his dead friend in her life eventually.

The pregnant patient lived some way out of town, and by the time Judd and Laurie reached the house, an apologetic father-to-be met them with the news that his wife's pains had stopped and she felt fine.

'She was worried that the baby was coming too

soon and we thought it best to call you out, Doctor. But it looks as if you've had a wasted journey.'

'This is Dr Whittaker, who's just joined the practice and will be looking after the baby when it does come,' said Judd as they got out of the car and turned towards the house. 'Now that we're here, we'll take a look at Mrs Cook and put both your minds at rest.'

The patient was thirty-five, late to be having her first baby, and naturally anxious, although she regularly attended the ante-natal clinic at the health centre and had been assured that there were no problems and that the baby was fine. Judd had told Laurie in the car that this was the third false alarm but that he continued to visit when asked because the one time that he failed to do so would probably be the one time that the baby chose to arrive early.

'Anxiety can play a big part in inducing false labour pains, as I told you before, Maureen,' he said as he replaced the uterine sounder in his bag. 'The baby may have been a little restless, but he isn't yet ready to come into the world, I promise.'

'I'm sorry to bring you all this way for nothing, Doctor,' she said contritely.

'All in a day's work.' He checked her blood-pressure and nodded approvingly. 'That's fine, and the baby's fine. But I think I'll see you once a week from now on, if that will make you feel more secure.'

'Oh, I think it will,' she said gratefully.

Laurie realised the personal touch that soothed a patient's fears, a vital part of any GP's workload, and wondered if she would be so successful in the coming months. She was still finding it a very different world from Hartlake, but it was one that she could easily make her home, she felt.

CHAPTER SIX

IT WAS late and Laurie felt weary as she slid into the passenger seat at Judd's side for the return journey in the dark.

He slotted a cassette into the car deck, and the murmuring music almost lulled her to sleep as the car traversed the quiet country roads. She didn't mind that he was obviously in no mood for conversation. Perhaps he was tired too. It was a relief that she didn't need to talk, to play any kind of role to please or interest him.

She was jolted awake as the car came to an abrupt halt, and only her seat-belt saved her from being thrown against the hard outlines of the dashboard. 'What's happened?' she exclaimed, startled.

Judd's expression was grim. 'Sorry, but we've just passed what looks like an accident—possibly a hit-and-run.' He reversed the car several yards along a deserted lane. 'Didn't you see the bike and the old man lying in the ditch?' He switched off the engine and reached to the back seat for his medical bag.

'I was half asleep,' she confessed, but he had already hurtled out of the car. Laurie hurried after him towards the elderly man who lay half in and half out of the ditch at the side of the road, muddied and bloodied.

Judd dropped to his knees beside the inert figure,

instantly seeking a pulse and then checking the man's pupils.

'These roads are used as racetracks by the local tearaways at this time of night, and they don't care who gets in the way,' he said grimly, running expert hands over the thin ribcage, craggy facial bones and greying head, while Laurie examined arms and legs for possible fractures.

She sat back on her heels, frowning. 'It doesn't look good.'

Judd unfurled his stethoscope to listen to the stertorous breathing and the cardiac rhythms then shook his head. 'No—and there isn't much we can do for him here. I'll call for an ambulance. . .*damn*! Edward took the mobile phone with him when he went out this afternoon, didn't he? That means a walk for one of us, I'm afraid.'

Straightening, he towered above Laurie for a moment, considering a plan of campaign, then he headed for the boot of the car, to return with a foil blanket and a torch.

'Stay with him while I alert the police and the Northwood General and get an ambulance sent out for him,' he ordered.

She bridled, resenting the summary allotment of responsibility. 'I can drive,' she reminded him crisply, unwilling to be left alone with an unconscious man in a steadily darkening lane. The hooligans who were presumably the cause of his condition might decide to come back to check on their victim, she thought with an apprehensive shiver. 'I suggest that *you* stay here and I'll go for assistance.' Her tone was firm.

'Do you know the location? Or the area? How to find Sadlers Farm, the nearest house with a telephone? What directions to give when you get through to the ambulance service? No? Then he's your baby until I get back. You can cope with the situation, surely?'

'Of course I can cope!' Stung by the impatient tone, the scornful slur on her professionalism, Laurie was far from admitting her unease.

'Then I'll leave you to do so.'

She watched the lights of the car recede with some trepidation. Looking about her, she disliked the threatening gloom of tall trees and high hedges and moonless night that surrounded her.

London, with its never-silent streets and easily available aid in any kind of emergency, suddenly seemed a very long way from her present situation.

Judd had left his medical bag with its supply of drugs and emergency equipment. Thankful for the torch, Laurie wrapped the foil blanket around the unconscious man and monitored his pulse and respiration as best she could while she waited for him to return.

There was the pungent smell of beer on the man's breath, some vomit mixed with blood on his shabby clothing, and he reeked to high heaven. The bundle untidily attached to the rear end of the battered, twisted bicycle indicated that he was a mobile gentleman of the road, pedalling around the country and seeking handouts wherever he could.

Having encountered many of his ilk during her Casualty days at Hartlake, Laurie wondered if he was more drunk than damaged. But Judd had shown concern, so maybe his clever hands had detected serious injury.

Crouching beside the comatose man, aware of furtive rustlings in the hedgerow and long grass that kept her weary senses on the stretch, she relaxed slightly when a brilliant moon emerged from behind a bank of dark cloud, although it cast an eerie light on her isolated vigil.

No other car passed her during the fifteen minutes or so before she heard the welcoming sound of Judd's Mercedes. In normal circumstances, she would have been too concerned with the patient's needs to count minutes, but out here in the middle of nowhere, with the surprisingly chill air clawing at her bare arms and face with clammy fingers and night sounds of birds and wild animals making her start, she almost fell on his neck with relief when the car roared to a halt.

He strode swiftly to her side.

'Ambulance and police are on their way,' he said reassuringly, having broken the speed limit in both directions in his haste to get back as soon as he could, more concerned about leaving her alone than he cared to admit. 'How is he? Any change?'

'Still unconscious and very cold,' she reported.

'Hypothermic. God knows how long he's been lying in this ditch, poor devil!'

As Laurie struggled to her feet, stiff and chilled, she turned the heel of her shoe on a tussock of grass, and Judd instinctively shot out both hands to steady her as she staggered against him, taking hold of her slender arms, looking down at the lovely face that seemed so wan and weary in the moonlight that it touched a chord of concern in his breast.

An urgent desire to wrap her around with his arms and seek solace for a long loneliness in the sweetness of her mouth and the enveloping enchantment of her body almost swamped every other consideration. Then she shivered, a tremble that swept her from head to toe.

'You're cold too,' he said abruptly. 'Go and sit in the car.' And he put both the girl and temptation away from him with a small, persuasive push.

Laurie stumbled towards the car in a daze, shaken to the core of her being by the powerful force that had emanated from him and the keen hunger in the lean, shadowed face as he gazed down at her for that brief, disturbing moment. Heart beating heavily, unevenly, she tingled all over with desire and disappointment.

Hastily, she blamed the moonlight that had bathed them both for the dangerous glitter in deep-set eyes and the imagined strain in his tense frame and handsome face, for that was surely safer than supposing he had been abruptly consumed with a longing akin to her own.

The siren of an approaching ambulance broke the silence of the night, and soon the injured man was aboard and carried off to hospital, while Judd dealt with the police officers who had arrived on the scene in response to his telephone call.

By the time all the formalities were completed and Judd was free to continue the drive back to Umber House, Laurie had gained control of her wayward emotions and determined to keep them on a tighter rein in future.

She *did* like Judd Harris, possibly more than was wise in the circumstances. His nearness and his touch had an immediate and alarming effect on her senses, but she suspected he still carried a brightly burning torch for his ex-wife. It was madness to teeter on the edge of loving him.

'We've been hearing all about your adventure last night,' Edward announced the next morning when Laurie looked into the kitchen before leaving for the surgery.

Judd looked at her over the golden head of the child who stood in the circle of his arm. 'You'll be pleased to hear that Alexander Arbuthnot Mackenzie is not only conscious but raising the roof about his damaged bike,' he said lightly.

Laurie lifted a sceptical eyebrow. 'I find it hard to believe he's in a fit state to raise the roof about anything. I didn't think he'd last the night!'

'He has eight stitches in his head and some bruised ribs, but X-rays show no fractures or internal injuries. He'll be kept in for a few days as he has a mild pneumonia, but he'll do.' He used the familiar term for patients expected to make a good recovery from illness or accident.

'A stroke of luck for the old codger that you happened along when you did.' Edward wondered if he only imagined a slight constraint between his partner and his pretty cousin.

'He'd have died in that ditch if we hadn't found him, certainly,' Laurie stated with conviction.

'I'm not so sure,' countered Judd. 'Don't under-estimate the survival factor of the type, Laurie. They're usually as tough as old boots—an apt comparison in Alexander's case, I gather. It seems he'd have thrown his ancient pair at Sister if they hadn't already been consigned to the incinerator. Something else that he's complaining about—vociferously!' he chuckled.

'Probably because he kept his entire fortune secreted in the soles,' Laurie said drily, from her experience of the shabby, shambling itinerants who frequented the streets of London and invariably turned up in the casualty department of Hartlake Hospital at one time or another.

Judd smiled. 'I believe they were thoroughly investigated before cremation, and his entire fortune amounts to four pounds and thirty-three pence,' he drawled.

Laurie didn't trust the twinkle in his blue eyes or the pleasing shock to her senses of his bewitching smile. She shook off the realisation that she found him too attractive and too exciting for comfort.

'Does he have any idea what happened to him?' she asked briskly.

'He says he was hit by a drunk-driver and found himself in the ditch. It's likely enough, but there's no evidence that any accident actually took place, according to our friends at the local police station.

So perhaps he was simply drunk and careering all over the road and fell off his bike.' Gently putting Jenefer to one side, Judd got to his feet. 'Anyway, I shall be looking in on him this morning and I'll let you have a progress report.'

'Thanks. I *am* interested,' she assured him. 'I hope to find time to visit him myself.'

A little to her disappointment, he ignored the carelessly dropped hint, and she was cross with herself for trying to manipulate some time in his company. What on earth was the matter with her? she wondered. It was less than a month since she had felt sure she loved Cris, and here she was hankering after another man!

Halfway through morning surgery, Laurie found herself without an important blood test result in a patient's notes. She buzzed the intercom without result and decided it would be quicker to slip along to the office and ask one of the medical secretaries if the result had actually come back from the path lab.

Excusing herself from the mother who nursed her anaemic five-year-old on her lap, she left the consulting-room and hurried along the corridor, to find that the desk in the reception area was temporarily unmanned. Patsy was talking to Judd, so deep in low-voiced conversation that she seemed unusually unaware of the buzz of the switchboard and a growing queue of patients.

The way Judd smiled at the receptionist who was also friend and neighbour and their meaningful body language as they stood close together just out of sight of patients appeared to tell its own story, and triggered a fierce shaft of dismay in Laurie's unprepared breast. But how absurd to mind their obvious closeness, she scolded herself sternly. *She* wasn't interested in Judd Harris!

Well, perhaps she was a teeny bit stirred by that potent mix of good looks and animal magnetism, if she was honest with herself. But she had no intention of entertaining the wistful, wanton thoughts of him.

For one thing, she liked Patsy, whose sunny nature made her a general favourite, and she was anxious not to tread on her toes. For another, it would be a mistake to fall for the first man she had met on her arrival in Umber, like some naïve first-year nurse yearning after a godlike consultant in the best tradition of romantic fiction!

As Judd turned from talking to Patsy and acknowledged her with a smiling nod, Laurie sternly suppressed the quickening of her senses in response to an age-old chemistry. But a tremor rippled through her as she recalled the fierce grip of her arms, the glow of intense emotion in his face and the current of almost electric awareness that had passed between them, leaving her in no doubt that he was conscious of the chemistry too.

She knew she hadn't imagined that sexual tension or the breathless excitement that had come into sudden, sharp focus. She accepted that such an attraction could blaze into being at a glance, a chance physical contact, entirely without wish or warning. But, like Judd who had also been burned in the past, she refused to accept the inevitability of being consumed by the flame.

In future, she must keep their relationship strictly professional. No more dinners or leisurely lunches or leaping at casual invitations to visit patients with him, Laurie told herself firmly. It was much too soon to feel that she could go overboard for him, but it was becoming more of a danger with every moment she spent with him.

Fortunately, Laurie soon discovered that moments alone with Judd were rare, possibly because he didn't seek such moments any more than she did—and possibly for much the same reasons.

She was rapidly absorbed into the household and the practice, made some friends and, in spite of the tart words thrown at Judd, felt in no hurry to leave the lovely old house in its beautiful setting that already felt like home. Umber House had enveloped her in the special spell of its charm.

Besides, moving out wouldn't free her from the special spell that Judd Harris seemed to cast on her with his smile and his touch and his enigmatic personality. She would continue to see him almost every day at the surgery, and she couldn't spend the rest of her life running from men who made too many demands on her emotions.

There seemed little need for her to do so in this instance, for Judd was obviously as determined as she was to maintain his distance. Courteous but unmistakably cool, he accepted her presence without appearing to welcome it particularly, a busy GP with so many friends and interests outside his work that it wasn't surprising that Laurie saw little of him.

She saw far more of Jamie, who attached himself

to her as if she provided an escape from Serene Lipski's well-meant mothering and Jenefer's natural bossiness. He was endearingly responsive to Laurie's affection and interest, and she welcomed the little boy's company, not least because it gave her an insight into the character and personality of the father he adored and tried to emulate.

Like Judd, Jamie was self-contained but warmly interested in everything, single-minded in his pursuits, wary of emotional involvement and yet suddenly and touchingly demonstrative at unexpected moments.

He was a caring child, concerned about the plight of the homeless and famine-stricken Third World countries, declaring his intention to be a doctor like Dad so he could make people well, insisting on sending his pocket money in response to a televised appeal for the victims of an earthquake in Central Asia, and then, like any other small boy, becoming more demon than angel in a sudden bout of naughtiness.

'Do you like it here, Laurie?' he wanted to know one evening with the directness that reminded her so much of Judd.

She realised that there was more than curiosity behind the question. 'Very much.' She put her arm about him as they sat side by side on the sofa in her cosy sitting-room, his reading book open between them.

'Then you won't go away?'

Detecting the anxious appeal, she drew Jamie into the warm curves of her body, moved by his need for reassurance and the way he had gravitated towards her since her arrival. 'I shall be here for a long time, Jamie,' she said firmly. Six months *was* a long time to a child, she knew.

'Till I'm grown up?' The words were muffled but urgent.

'Till you're almost grown up, anyway,' Laurie compromised, hugging him tightly.

'Please don't make promises you aren't likely to keep,' Judd said harshly, from the open doorway. 'He's had too many disappointments.'

The brusque words shattered the intimacy of the regular half-hour before bedtime that Laurie tried to share with Jamie, and she turned to frown a warning. 'Seven *is* almost grown up,' she countered firmly, ignoring the disapproval in his narrowed eyes, aware that Jamie couldn't imagine himself as old as seven. His birthday fell at Christmas, just before she was due to make a decision whether to leave Umber or stay on as a partner in the practice.

'Time for your bath, Jamie. Jenefer's been looking everywhere for you.' Judd ruffled his son's bright hair, and Jamie obediently scrambled down from the sofa, impulsively stretched to plant a kiss on Laurie's cheek, then ran out of the room.

She closed the reading book. 'Jenefer knows that he's usually up here with me at this time,' she said mildly.

'I hope he isn't being a pest.' Judd knew he should follow his son, but he was rooted to the spot by the warm, sensual beauty of the girl who lay back against the sofa cushions to look up at him, her loosened hair cascading about her face in a dark cloud, the unconscious provocation of peeping breasts at the plunge of her silk shirt riveting his gaze and kindling the quick-fired desire of a strongly sensual man.

It was just the swamping reaction to her unconscious sexuality that drove him from the house to spend his off-duty hours at the golf course or sailing or playing squash or bridge with friends—anything but remain within sight and sound of the temptation that this girl had for him, he admitted ruefully.

'We have a lot of fun together,' Laurie said lightly. 'I help him with his reading and he's teaching me to fish.' As she smiled up at him, she almost choked on a sudden flood of wild yearning. Hastily she held out Jamie's book, hoping the flush of desire hadn't invaded her own face with give-away warmth. 'He's forgotten this, and he'll need it for school tomorrow. . .'

The words sounded slightly strangled to her own ears, and she swallowed. How dreadful to want him so much, to feel wave upon wave of uninvited longing sweep through her, to be so tempted to draw him down to her aching arms. She tried desperately to stifle and suppress the invading emotions.

Judd took the book from her, almost but not quite brushing her fingers in a deliberate bid for physical contact. It took all his control to resist the insane impulse to seize her hand and draw her up and into the embrace for which he hungered.

Like Jamie, he needed her warmth and sweetness and generous affection. But he knew the dangers of her attractions, whereas Jamie, child that he was, only knew the urgent need for the love and the interest that Laurie seemed so willing to provide.

He didn't want his small son to become too attached, for he was vulnerable, still suffering from an undeserved desertion, seeking a substitute for the love and need that had been denied him by an uncaring mother. Judd was anxious for Jamie, afraid Laurie might not welcome or value the gift of a little boy's love. More important, she wouldn't be around forever—and wasn't that what Jamie needed more than anything else? The stability and the security of being loved for the rest of his life, come what may?

It didn't occur to him that he listed the reasons for his own reluctance to become too fond of the lovely Laurie Whittaker.

'It's good of you to give him so much of your time,' he said stiffly. 'But he ought to be with Jenefer or Kay or the boys he knows at school. He's had too much adult company.'

Laurie sat up, visibly dismayed. 'Are you telling me to discourage him? To spend less time with him?'

Judd steeled his resolve. 'I don't want his obvious dependence on you becoming dangerous,' he told her bluntly. 'After all, you may well be gone by the end of the year.'

She jumped to her feet, smarting at the implication that he wouldn't lift a finger to keep her from leaving. 'You can't protect him from the pain of loving, Judd! He'll learn like the rest of us that if you give even a small part of your heart to someone there's a chance that they won't want it, then or ever!' Strangely, she wasn't thinking of Cris as she voiced the bitter words.

Seeing the shadow that crossed her face, hearing the hurt in her lilting voice, Judd put a hand on her shoulder in silent sympathy. It was a mistake. Her nearness, her drifting perfume and the silk of her skin invoked a relentless stab of desire and she was suddenly in his arms.

He had meant only to comfort. So he wasn't sure why he kissed her.

CHAPTER SEVEN

THE world spun and then stood breathlessly still as strong arms enveloped her and she met the brick wall of Judd's tall, powerful body. His warm, seeking mouth covered her own and Laurie was engulfed in the fierce tide of passion in his kiss.

Briefly, unsure but filled with wanting, she hesitated, but he was a rock of reassurance, and she melted into him, giving him kiss for kiss.

His gentle hands moved over her, pressing her close, promising unbelievable delights with their sure, stroking touch, and she was lost to all but the moment, the sweet intoxication of desire in her veins. Eager for the paradise he promised with his kiss and his ardent, muscular body, she had no thought for the afterwards, only the passionate present, as Judd swept her down to the deep cushions of the sofa.

As consumed as she was by the tidal flood of emotion, his kiss became deeper, longer, even more demanding. A hot light in the blue eyes that searched her ecstatic, dreaming face for objection and found none, he unbuttoned her blouse with unsteady fingers to expose breasts that he tenderly cupped and then kissed, and Laurie sighed, almost swooning, stroking the proud head and the nape of his neck and his strong shoulder with fluttering, caressing fingers.

She arched on a small moan of pleasure as his lips traced the still-vivid line between pale and bronzed flesh and then teased the pert pink tips of her nipples with a skill that sent flames shooting and dancing and piercing the very epicentre of her being.

She wound her arms fiercely about his neck as he brought up his head to kiss her tremulous mouth, and knew that wanting him was the greatest force she had ever encountered.

His touch was sheer magic and his kiss was heaven, and she thrilled in joyous anticipation as his skilful, sensual mouth and hands and body set her clamouring for the thrust of powerful and pleasuring flesh. She was ready to give and go on giving with a wild, joyous abandon she had never known before.

Lost to the world and everything in it, she drew him down, down, ever closer. . .

She uttered a gasping cry.

Judd swore, struck out in sudden, frustrated fury, and on a startled bark and a whimper Angelo scrabbled and slithered to the floor in bewilderment at their unfriendly reception of his unannounced decision to join them on the sofa.

Judd's handsome face darkened with anger. 'Damn dog! I should have shut the bloody door!' he exploded wrathfully.

At the scowling growl of his tone, Angelo's tail went down between his legs and he slunk towards the door he had widened with his thrusting body as he padded silently into the room.

It wasn't really funny, but Laurie couldn't help laughing as she hastily sat up clutching at her blouse and fumbling with the buttons, all desire abruptly knocked out of her by the descent of the dog's heavy body as he leaped over the back of the sofa.

Judd had never felt less like laughing, still tense, still trembling with heightened passion, still astonished by the speed and the strength of the overwhelming wanting that had swept aside everything but desire, and his scowl deepened and his heart hardened as he saw Laurie's widely smiling mouth and sparkling eyes and seemingly unruffled composure.

It was evident that the tender urgency of those moments had meant little to an obviously experienced girl. No doubt she looked upon it as just a casual encounter between two people irresistibly attracted to each other, he thought grimly, furious with himself for thinking of it as unforgettable.

'Oh, don't scold him!' Laurie begged as he vented his fury on the bewildered animal. 'He wasn't to know. . .and we weren't being sensible, Judd. It could have been anyone coming into the room—Jamie, for instance!'

As her blood cooled and reason returned, she was horrified to realise the risks they had taken, making love on her sofa like a couple of irresponsible teenagers swept by passions they couldn't control. She must have been momentarily mad to sink into that glorious sea of swooning sensation in his arms and be so ready to surrender her virginity to a man she scarcely knew when she had denied Cris so consistently. Perhaps she had never loved Cris so passionately, after all. Or at all!

'There's no privacy in this house,' Judd agreed in

angry frustration. 'Children and animals wander in and out of rooms at their pleasure.'

He wondered how she could treat it so lightly when their relationship had suddenly taken such a serious turn. Why wasn't she as dismayed and as disappointed as himself? Had she been less aroused than she led him to suppose when she had wound her arms about him, kissed him so ardently, responded with a sweetness that could sweep a man into loving all unawares?

Bitterly he cursed the weakness in himself that had succumbed to the attractions of that lovely face and warmly welcoming arms, creating problems for the future. For how could they continue to work together, share the same roof, behave as if nothing had happened?

Laurie smiled up at him, sensing the depth and the disappointment of his anger. She was disappointed too, but also relieved that Angelo had prevented a total surrender to the dictates of desire. For she wanted to mean more to Judd Harris than just another casual, too easy conquest.

She almost wished he hadn't made that irresistible overture, turning their comfortable relationship on its head. But it wasn't possible to turn back the clock. They could only go forward into a future that might hold friendship at least and possibly a happiness that eradicated the painful past for them both.

She put a comforting hand on his arm. 'Never mind, Judd. Next time we'll make sure the door is locked,' she said lightly.

His eyes narrowed with instant dislike of the warm

sexual promise in her smiling eyes and voice. What had happened between them had surely been spontaneous, an incandescent flame leaping to consume them both. So it offended him to hear her speak of 'next time' in cold blood.

He shook off her lingering hand to discourage her from supposing that his sudden, overwhelming desire for her had been the preliminary to an affair. For in the midst of embracing her, kissing her, coaxing her towards surrender, he had experienced a rush of tenderness that he recognised as the first kindling of love, and he had no intention of treading that perilous path again. His penchant for this pretty girl with her shining sapphire eyes and soft mouth and beautiful body must be nipped in the bud now!

'There won't be a next time, Laurie. I'm keeping well away from you in future. You're too rich for my blood,' he said sardonically, deliberately setting out to end what should never have begun. For good measure, he added, 'I know you're missing your boyfriend, but it isn't a good idea to snatch at the first substitute that comes along.'

The mocking words and the piercing chill of accusing eyes shocked and dismayed Laurie, and she stepped back in consternation. 'Damn you!' she flared in justifiable anger. '*You* grabbed *me*!'

His smile flicked her with the sting of amused scorn. 'You weren't averse to being grabbed, as I recall,' he drawled. 'But it was a mistake that I won't repeat.'

She coloured, unable to deny the accusation but determined not to be branded a wanton by a man who had made all the running. 'You're an attractive man,' she conceded coolly, her eyes flashing fury and her chin on the tilt. 'And I *do* miss Cris—just as you miss your wife. We both lost our heads for a moment. No big deal, was it? But I do agree with you that it doesn't have to happen again.' Her slender body was stiff with anger.

'It won't,' Judd assured her grimly.

'No. Who needs that kind of complication?'

The quiver of her mouth belied the proud stare and the defiance in her tone. Knowing he had hurt her, Judd felt a repentant catch at his heart. 'Look, Laurie. . .'

She was never to know what he might have said, for Serene burst into the room, breathless from a hurried ascent of the stairs, a hand pressed to her breast to alleviate the discomfort of haste and anxiety.

'Judd! Jamie said you were up here! Can you come and look at Marcus? He's so hot and he keeps being sick, and he's such an awful colour.' Her voice caught. 'I'm sure something's very wrong. . .'

Alerted by a mother's usually infallible instinct, their own concerns forgotten for the time being, both Judd and Laurie sped in the woman's wake as she hurried back to the Blue Room.

Marcus was intermittently crying and coughing, and Jenefer bent over him, uttering soothing noises. Jamie stood by the door, looking anxious, alarmed by the flurry of activity, and Laurie put a comforting arm about him.

Judd scooped the choking baby from his cot and

Marcus whimpered in obvious distress before sicking all over his shirt. 'It doesn't matter. It happens all the time. I'm used to it,' Judd declared with the impatience of professional concern as Serene mopped at him with a handful of tissues, exclaiming apologies.

But shortly he handed the baby to Laurie and went into the connecting bathroom to clean up, and she took the opportunity to examine Marcus for herself. Burning with fever, feebly turning his head from the light, he uttered pathetic wails of protest as she looked into his eyes and ears and mouth, felt the painfully swollen glands in his neck and gently moved stiff, resisting limbs.

'He isn't *well*,' she understated, fearing that he was very ill indeed. 'I think we should have him admitted to hospital for a few days, just to be on the safe side. One can't be too careful with premature babies, as you know.' She smiled gently at the hovering Serene. 'Even a mild dose of flu or a chest infection can be a serious setback if it isn't properly treated.'

'Do you think that's all it is—just flu or something like it?' The mask of slightly superior cool had slipped to reveal a panicking mother like any other in similar circumstances.

'Probably,' Laurie lied comfortingly. 'A viral infection of some kind, anyway.' As a shirtless Judd came to the door, muscles rippling in a bronzed bare chest as he dried his hands on a towel, she shot him a glance that she was thankful to note he interpreted correctly.

As he sent her an almost imperceptible nod of agreement, she knew that meningitis was the first thought that had leaped to his mind too, but he agreed with her that there was no need to alarm Serene at this stage.

'We won't bother with an ambulance,' he said as if there was no need for urgency. 'I'll just put on a clean shirt while you put some things in a case for yourself, as you'll obviously want to stay with Marcus. Then I'll take you both to the Northwood. Laurie won't mind putting the chilren to bed and staying with them until Edward or I get back.'

'Of course not.' In fact, Laurie was taken aback by the high-handed assumption, but she didn't protest. It didn't seem a suitable moment to remind him that *she* was the paediatrician, with far more experience of such cases, and it was obvious from Serene's grateful face that Judd's company and support would be preferable to her own.

Left alone with the two children and the task of diverting their minds and her own from the anxiety about Marcus and getting them into bed, she found her thoughts kept turning to Judd and the way he had looked and the stringency in his deep voice that had destroyed all the magic of those moments in his arms.

What had she done to deserve his censure. . .except put her arms about him and give him her lips and very nearly her body, as he had seemed to desire? His unexpected, hurtful reaction convinced her that he had been disappointed or disgusted by her too-eager response. But she *wasn't* a wanton! She had been as surprised as Judd by the fiery passion evoked by his kiss and his touch.

She sighed.

Jenefer twisted to look at her doubtfully. 'Is Marcus very ill?' Her underlip wobbled slightly.

Like her beautiful mother, she was only serene on the surface, Laurie realised with sudden insight. Beneath the placid exterior and confident bossiness was a little girl desperately needing to be reassured.

'He's being well looked after, darling,' she soothed as she unbraided the silky, flaxen hair, ready to brush it into shining candy-floss before Jenefer climbed into the turned-back bed.

'But he's in hospital, isn't he? Daddy went to hospital and never came home again.'

No wonder the poor child was alarmed, Laurie thought compassionately. People talked glibly of the resilience of childhood, the ease of acceptance, but she had treated a number of children bereaved of a parent and knew the traumas, the bewilderment and pain, that could be concealed with chatter and play.

'That won't happen to Marcus,' she said firmly.

'Is Dr Judd looking after him?'

Laurie hugged her warmly, knowing that she loved and trusted Judd. She felt it might be dangerously easy for her to love and trust him too—then she brushed the thought aside. For how could she want a man who had treated her so shabbily, spoken so harshly, rejected her so brutally? It would be hard enough simply to live beneath the same roof with him!

'And some very nice nurses, I expect,' she said lightly.

Jenefer digested the assurance. Then she demanded, 'Why aren't *you* looking after Marcus? Mummy says that you're the baby doctor.' She peeped through her fall of blonde hair, hesitating. 'Do you help babies to get born, Dr Laurie?'

'Sometimes.'

The little girl pleated folds in her pink nightdress with pudgy fingers. 'Does it hurt the babies?'

Laurie cradled the plump, anxious face. 'Not in the slightest, Jenefer,' she assured her.

'Marcus was hurt and couldn't come home with Mummy,' Jenefer challenged instantly.

'Marcus was in a hurry to be born. He rushed into the world, just as impatient as most little boys, and had to stay in hospital for a few days to make sure that he'd brought all his bits and bobs with him,' Laurie explained lightly, and was rewarded with a slightly naughty giggle.

'Do you have any babies, Dr Laurie?'

'Not yet.'

There was a brief, considering pause. 'Don't you *want* any?'

Laurie loved children, but she had been too busy doctoring their various ills in recent years to give much thought to motherhood. It was only since she had come to live in Umber House and become so involved with Jamie that her maternal instincts had been allowed full rein. She hadn't known they were so strong.

'One day,' she returned, and Jenefer seemed

satisfied. She pushed her gently towards the bed. 'In you get, sweetheart—and straight to sleep like a good girl. When you wake up in the morning you'll probably find that Marcus is much, much better.'

She tucked her in, standing in for the absent Serene, and bent over to set a last kiss on the flushed cheek. As two plump arms flew up to wind themselves about her neck, Laurie felt she didn't deserve the affectionate embrace, for she had given far more of her time and attention to Jamie than Jenefer since her arrival.

That was the danger of assuming too much from an outward show of self-sufficiency, she admitted wryly. Jamie had turned to her, reached out to her, clung when she allowed him into her heart, while Jenefer stood on the sidelines, wistful but unable to admit her needs.

Laurie was tempted to wonder if Judd shared a similar trait.

Closing the bedroom door on the already drowsy little girl, she thought of Cris and the children they might have had if things had worked out—and suddenly knew, on a penetrating shaft of reason unclouded by emotion, that he wasn't a man she would want to father her unborn children.

He was a brilliant surgeon, but selfish, wrapped up in himself and his wishes and his work, so ambitious that she doubted there was room in his life for a wife, let alone children.

Whereas Judd. . .

She hastily shied from the wistful fancy that had taken her so completely by surprise. But he was a good father, loving and kind but firm, finding time to enjoy a variety of interests and activities with Jamie, and he had done an excellent job of bringing him up in spite of the difficulties of combining single parenthood with his very demanding job.

He was good with all children. Having seen him with small patients at the surgery and observed their relaxed response to the smiling concern in his kind eyes and the gentle touch and the warm compassion in his quiet voice, Laurie knew it was at such moments that she liked him best.

Unexpectedly, she had a vision of a baby with a cluster of dark curls like her own and a warm mouth and brilliantly blue eyes inherited from a very handsome father. Shaken, fired with a longing that was becoming too frequent and too familiar, she swept the thought out of her mind, but it persisted, came back even more strongly later when she answered a frightened cry from Jamie's room and cuddled him close to comfort him.

Waking from a bad dream, he was crying and clinging and muddled, confusing her with the mummy he couldn't remember and, probably, the various mummies who had replaced her for short periods in the intervening years. Laurie felt a foolish twinge of jealousy of those unknown women in Judd's past.

Bringing Jamie from his bed, she sat in a chair by the window with him in her lap, crooning nursery rhymes and silly, soothing songs until he was over his fright, and it was then that she saw again in her mind's eye the child she would dearly love to bear.

Judd's child, like the boy she cradled so tenderly and could never have abandoned if she had been his mother.

He was such an engaging, heart-stealing little boy. Laurie had quite fallen in love with him. There were sobering moments, such as now, when she wondered if she was falling in love with the father too.

That was enchantment of a different kind. The warmth in a sudden smile, the understanding in a shared glance, the occasional glimpse of humour or the hint of tenderness in a touch could catch and toss and startle her unsuspecting heart and fill her with the melt of longing.

Her heart must be very fickle, or else she had never really cared for Cris. Or was it only that she had finally discovered the ecstasy to be found in a man's ardent embrace? Judd *was* ardent. She only had to look into those compelling eyes to sense the passion in him, a passion to which her wilful body had responded all too readily—and given him quite the wrong impression of her, she thought ruefully.

As she mused, Judd's shadow fell across them, his tall, impressive body outlined in the doorway by the light from the corridor, and Laurie put a warning finger to her lips as the heaviness of Jamie's head on her breast and the floppiness of his sturdy limbs told her that he slept.

'He woke and wanted you,' she said softly, thinking that it spoke volumes that a small boy called out for Daddy rather than Mummy when he stirred in the night. 'I think he'd been dreaming.'

'He has the occasional nightmare, like most children. Here, give him to me—he's heavy.' Judd moved to take his son as she struggled to her feet with his dead weight clasped to her slight frame.

'Don't wake him!' Judd stood very close as she transferred Jamie into his strong arms. His exciting male scent was pungent in her nostrils, and she was suddenly weak with foolish, feverish wanting, remembering the urgent need of each other—so short a time ago but an eternity as far as he was concerned, she realised with a sinking heart. Not a flicker of shared or remembered sensation showed in that lean, attractive face.

Heart and senses on the leap, she clutched at her composure as well as her yellow silk kimono, having meant to shower and settle down with a book until Judd returned with news of Marcus.

Judd covered Jamie with the duvet as he muttered and nestled into the pillows, sinking deeper into sleep. 'I'm grateful to you for coming in,' he said stiffly, shamed by the recollection of his harshness, the deliberate contempt with which he had whipped her, in the face of her concern for his son.

He was trying to forget the somersault of his heart as he had looked into the room and saw her curled in the big chair with Jamie in her lap. It had been a poignant glimpse of life as it might have been for Jamie and himself if Marla had been blessed with such a warm, generous nature, and its effect had been so unexpected and so staggering that he wasn't ready to consider its implications. . .

CHAPTER EIGHT

LAURIE felt rebuffed by the chilly tone. 'Is Serene still at the hospital?' she asked, falling back on the impersonal.

'For the time being. She's very concerned about Marcus, naturally.' With the lightest, briefest touch of her arm, Judd indicated that they should adjourn to the corridor. Laurie obediently moved ahead of him, silk swishing about her delicately curved body, and he followed her from the room, not quite closing the door.

Laurie was concerned too. The baby was so tiny, so frail, so heart-catchingly sweet, stirring all the instincts that had led her into paediatrics, and she had fretted all evening because someone other than herself was in charge, examining, diagnosing and prognosing, ordering the necessary tests and prescribing medication and monitoring his condition.

Waiting and wondering and worrying was more stressful than actually doing something for a sick child. But perhaps concern for Marcus wasn't her only reason for lingering to talk to Judd, if she was honest with herself.

'How *is* Marcus?' she asked.

'Still very distressed. He's in an oxygen tent and Curtis has ordered the routine tests for meningitis—that *is* what you suspected, isn't it?'

'So did you,' Laurie said quickly.

He nodded. 'The symptoms point in that direction. The devil of it is that we may be worrying Serene for no good reason. It may just be a viral infection that will clear with antibiotics. But I had to warn her that it could be something more serious.'

'He *is* a prem, and I must say I feel happier that he's in hospital with all the right equipment on hand if anything goes wrong. I expect Serene will want to stay with him while there's some cause for anxiety, so someone will have to look after the house and the children in the meantime. And I'm a woman, so no doubt it falls to me,' she finished flatly.

Judd shrugged. 'We managed without you in the past.' He didn't add that while life before Laurie had been hectic at times, it hadn't offered a constant assault on his emotions.

But it was certainly in his mind.

'I didn't mean that the way it sounded,' Laurie said hastily, seeing the steel in his blue eyes and knowing that he had misconstrued her attitude to the inevitable. The last thing she wanted was to disappoint him in any way! 'You know I'll do whatever I can, wherever I'm needed. We're a team, after all. . .'

She smiled up at him, a little shy, a little unsure, longing to reach out to him as her aching arms and thudding heart prompted. The way he had rebuffed her earlier, so brutal and so undeserving, kept her from plunging into total folly, however.

Judd looked down at her in the dimly lit corridor, fighting for control, aware of longing in his heart and hunger in his loins. The hush of the big house surrounded them with an aura of romance and mystery, for there were numerous ghosts, phantoms of those men and women from bygone days who had lived and loved beneath its gabled roof. He doubted that any one of those long-dead men could have wanted any woman as ardently as he desired Laurie in that still moment.

Barefooted, swathed in rustling yellow silk, she barely came up to his broad shoulder. She looked up at him with the shy half-smile that he found so appealing, the wistful oval of her face pale and pretty amid the tumbling dark curls, slender body in the thin wrapper inclining towards him with an invitation that might or might not be conscious but was certainly undeserved.

Manfully, he resisted the almost irresistible temptation to sweep her into his arms, to enfold her with his desire, to take moist, slightly parted lips and urge her into the sweet giving that he craved. For she was lovely, enchanting, and he feared he would want to hold her and keep her close to his side forever. . .

Laurie sensed an atmosphere so electric that it was tangible, and her pulses quickened. She wondered if Edward had come in with him or stayed to support Serene if the baby's condition should suddenly worsen.

Was she alone with Judd in this silent, darkened house except for the sleeping children? Was his heart hammering as heavily as her own? Was his body stirring, clamouring, as urgently as her own in that breathless moment? Or did she only imagine the weighty awareness, the throbbing tension, the urgency of mutual need?

Time stood still for them both as heads and hearts whirled in an eddy of excitement and yearning. But neither could or would make the first move that would hurtle them into each other's arms and cement the ineradicable shift in their relationship.

Judd spoke, breaking the spell that seemed to bewitch and bind them with an age-old magic. 'I'm afraid none of this is working out the way you expected,' he said with a gesture that embraced all that had happened between them as well as the unsettled domestic situation.

Laurie shrugged. 'I'm not really sure what I expected. . .' Certainly not the impact that this proud, self-sufficient, often austere man was having on her emotions, the rush of blood to head and heart, the mad, mad longing to belong to him for the rest of her life, she thought ruefully.

It was crazy, illogical, even more foolish than believing herself in love with Cris, who had never loved anyone in his life. For this was a man who made no secret of the fact that he had never stopped loving the woman who had let him and Jamie down so badly.

'But you're wishing you'd turned down Edward's invitation,' he suggested with wry understanding in his eyes.

'I haven't quite reached that stage.' She moved from his disturbing proximity and what it was doing to her wayward senses. 'But a few days of cooking and cleaning might just send me hotfoot back to Hartlake!'

Her lilting laugh drifted back along the corridor as she left him, heading for her room, and Judd looked after her, wrenched with a sense of loss that he scarcely understood, and wondering if she would welcome a really valid reason to rush back to London and all her friends and the man who was possibly the great love of her life.

No doubt she *was* missing him, just as she had claimed with those defiant words, and no doubt the ache of loneliness had driven her into the arms of a man who meant no more than an ease for hunger, a balm for hurt pride. Judd understood. He had been there himself. He remembered the hurt and the desolation, the bitter anger at the waste of loving where it wasn't wanted, the snatch at any kind of solace for the pain.

Now nothing remained of that long-ago upheaval of his life but anger. A man couldn't live forever with a shattered dream, and he had long since accepted that Marla was never coming back to him and Jamie.

At long last, he was sure he didn't want her back. In fact, he was ready to love again, to trust again. All he needed was a warm, caring woman who believed as he did that loving was a commitment for life. Someone who would take Jamie into her heart as well as himself and turn them into a family.

He was tempted to believe that Laurie fitted the bill to perfection, but Edward had said that her dedication to medicine had wrecked her romance with the Hartlake surgeon, and Judd had seen for himself how much she gave to her work and her patients. He shrank instinctively from any kind of emotional involvement with a woman whose first love was and might always be her career.

He didn't need another Marla in his life. . .

Laurie laughed as she left him outside Jamie's room, but she felt more like crying, and it took all her strength of mind not to give way to the choking tears when she reached the sancturary of her attic rooms. For her heart and body were heavy with disappointment.

Would it have hurt him to apologise, even indirectly? All it took was a friendly word, one warm smile—and she was more than willing to forgive and forget. Damn his arrogance and the indifference that set up a brick wall between them! It was all very well for Judd to act as if he had never held her and kissed her so passionately, but *she* was still tingling—and his sudden revulsion of feeling was indelibly etched on her humiliated heart. . .

She warmed the metal sounding-piece of her stethoscope between her hands while she talked to the young father who had brought his baby girl to the surgery for examination next morning.

'It's her chest, Doctor,' he said anxiously. 'It never seems to clear, and she's always catching colds. And she wheezes with every breath.'

Laurie nodded. 'I'm glad you brought her to the surgery. Let me have a listen to her chest and perhaps we can find out what's causing all these colds.'

She smiled at the toddler, who sat on her daddy's lap, looking the picture of health in spite of the congestion that Laurie could hear in her respiration. The rosy flush and over-bright eyes could be deceptive, a sign of illness rather than good health.

'If Daddy lifts up your vest, will you let me put my stethoscope on your chest, Miranda?' she asked brightly. 'When I've had a listen to what's going on inside you, I'll let you have a listen too, if you like.'

'She doesn't like doctors,' Mr Murray warned with something in his tone that conveyed that his own distrust of the medical profession was more to the point.

'Oh, I'm sure she knows that doctors are nice people who like to make people feel better. Don't you, Miranda?' Laurie appealed to the child in the gently reassuring tone that usually eased the fears of her smaller patients.

As the three-year-old nodded her head and lifted up her vest before her daddy could do it, Laurie knew she had won the toddler's confidence, and she hastened to listen to the informative rumbles and whistles conveyed by the affected lungs.

Experience, together with other symptoms that the father detailed in response to her questions, made her suspect that this was an undetected case of cystic fibrosis that needed specialist confirmation.

Further questioning elicited the fact that Miranda's mother could be a carrier of the inherited condition and that she was already pregnant with her second child. Laurie did her best to convince Mr Murray that his daughter needed to see a specialist as soon as possible in the face of his repeated demands for some medicine to clear Miranda's chest and his insistence that she was just prone to colds, as his mother said he had been as a baby.

Eventually he agreed to take the child to the Northwood General when he received a letter of appointment from the chest clinic, and Laurie breathed a sigh of relief as he went from the consulting-room, clutching the prescription she had written to satisfy his obvious feeling that 'a nice drop of linctus' could work miracles.

She squeezed in a visit to the hospital to see Marcus between morning surgery and a trip to the supermarket. All week she had been busy with looking after the children, cooking and cleaning and fitting in surgery hours and a number of house calls to lighten Edward's workload, and she had had to rely on her cousin for news of the baby.

He was still very poorly, but the results of the initial tests indicated that it was a viral infection rather than the meningitis they had all dreaded.

Laurie was vividly reminded of her years at Hartlake as she walked into the paediatric ITU with its cots and incubators and high-tech equipment, its drip stands and bleeping monitors and sterile-clad nurses. She paused at the nursing station for a word with the sister, who instantly gave her permission to enter the ward and provided her with a gown and mob-cap.

The balding young consultant turned from his examination of a sleepy Marcus to look at her intently as she approached. She had expected to be challenged, and a smile was already shaping her lips.

'I know you, don't I?' He creased an already furrowed brow.

'I don't think we've met.' About to extend a hand and announce her name, Laurie paused in sudden, startled recognition. 'Yes, we have! It's Michael Curtis, isn't it? I didn't realise—oh, the name rang a bell, of course. But it's been years. . . How are you?'

It *was* years, and he had only been a casual acquaintance briefly encountered in ward or clinic, a senior registrar with rather more hair in the days when she was still struggling with her finals. But he had been a good friend of Crispin Page in those days and was possibly still in touch with him. She experienced a moment of panic at the thought that he might tell Cris she was in Umber and he'd come looking for her and disrupt her emotions all over again.

As if it was likely, she told herself cynically. Cris had already forgotten all about her, no doubt!

'I'm fine—and you look marvellous, Laurie. Absolutely glowing.' His tone was warmly admiring. He made a careful note on the chart and handed it to the staff nurse, who hooked it over the end of the cot. 'So you've left Hartlake to join our bustling community, have you? I gather you've joined Edward Fenton's practice.'

Laurie was relieved that the careless tone conveyed no hint that he knew all about her romance with Cris and its abrupt ending and her resultant decision to leave London.

'We're cousins,' she explained. 'His practice

needed a paediatrician and I needed a change. It seemed a good match.'

Michael nodded. 'Well, it's very nice to see you again,' he said absently, his attention already reverting to his busy round and the waiting staff nurse. 'We must have dinner one evening and you can bring me up to date on the Hartlake news.'

'I'd like that,' she assured him politely, but she felt an evening in his company would be an evening spent avoiding the subject of Cris, and that wasn't her idea of a good time.

'Are you here to see a patient, or——?'

'This one.' She indicated the snuffling, restless baby with his flushed countenance and the twitching limbs that protested at the presence of intravenous drips and monitor wires. She bent to stroke damp wisps of hair from the hot forehead and smile into puzzled, baby-blue eyes. 'How is he?'

'Not at all well, I'm afraid,' said Michael. 'The infection was fairly widespread by the time he was admitted, and then he had a bad reaction to the antibiotics. I'm trying a new drug to bring down his temperature and heighten his resistance to further infection. But it will take a day or two before we can see results.'

'But it definitely isn't meningitis?'

Michael reached for the case file and took out the reports from the path lab. 'All negative, as you see. But it's a nasty little bug with similar effects, so it was an understandable conclusion to draw. Is he your patient, Laurie?'

'Not exactly. His mother is my cousin's housekeeper. As she lives in, we were on the scene when Marcus became so ill.'

'Housekeeper? That gorgeous blonde with the terrific legs?' The amorous gleam in his eyes betrayed that he shared a keen interest in the opposite sex with Cris. 'I'd have gone into general practice if I'd known that was one of the perks!' He grinned.

'She's more a friend of the family than a housekeeper,' Laurie hastened to explain. 'She's recently lost her husband, and Edward offered her a home until she feels more settled.'

Michael turned to the hovering staff nurse and took a syringe from the kidney dish she held, then bent over Marcus.

'If her cooking is only half as good as she looks then she's the woman I've been looking for all these years,' he said whimsically, expertly injecting another dose of antibiotic into his small patient. He dropped the used syringe into the dish and gently massaged the tiny buttocks. Marcus registered indignation and he touched a long finger to the small palm of an angrily waving hand. 'Your mummy's a cracker, young man,' he said warmly. In answer to Laurie's warning nudge, he smiled over his shoulder at the approaching Serene, not at all abashed that the light-hearted words had obviously been overheard. 'Good morning, Mrs Lipski. I'm not very popular at the moment. Your baby's just had another injection and, as you can hear, he isn't too pleased about it. . .'

Laurie smiled at Serene and stood aside to allow her to stand beside her baby's cot and talk to the consultant in charge of his case. It had been an anxious few days for her, she knew, waiting for the results of tests and treatment, watching for the least sign of improvement or deterioration, only leaving the ward to eat or snatch a few hours of sleep.

She looked tired and rather strained but as immaculately groomed as ever, blonde hair in its sleek, shining coil and make-up perfectly applied.

Laurie wondered how she found the time! *She* had been almost too busy to do more than whisk a comb through her dark curls and wash her face, she thought wryly.

Edward was profusely grateful for everything she did. Judd seemed to take it for granted that she would strain every nerve and stretch every sinew to make life easier for him and his partner.

It was exactly what she *was* doing, but his continued coolness frequently tempted her to down tools. However, Jamie's clinging dependence and Jenefer's shy affection prevented such an impulsive gesture. For she couldn't desert the children, even at the risk of sinking deeper into the dangerous waters of wanting a man who kept her at a determined distance.

What was it about her that made men so reluctant to get deeply involved? First Cris—and now Judd. And why did it matter so much? she chided herself. For she had her work, her ambitions, her future in medicine. Who needed men? she asked herself flippantly.

But she couldn't seem to forget the warm tenderness of Judd's mouth and the sensuous scorch of his breath on her bare breast, the heady, aching desire to give herself utterly to the delights and demands of his embrace.

It was wanton, almost wicked, but she lay awake at night, wanting him, thinking of him just a flight of stairs away, perhaps wanting her too, and too proud or too stubborn to admit it. Only the fear of another rebuff kept Laurie safely in her room at such times, she knew, shocked but unashamed.

For why should it always be the man who took what he wanted and walked away, unmoved? Why shouldn't she admit to the breathless longing for a man who stirred her so deeply at a touch? And why should she call it love when it was probably nothing of the kind? she thought defiantly.

With a car boot stacked with groceries, Laurie stopped off at the surgery with a message for Edward and saw Judd in the car park, talking to a district nurse, his good looks and unconscious charm having its usual effect.

The girl preened and fluttered and flirted in automatic response, and Laurie's heart contracted with a little alarm as she wondered if he admired the bubbly Nurse Davis, who was very pretty, very popular with the patients and, according to Patsy, blatantly interested in the handsome physician.

Judd glanced at her as she walked towards the building. For a brief moment their eyes met and held, and Laurie felt her heart wrench with a sudden longing. She smiled at him with impulsive warmth that tried to remind him of the intimate encounter that had been so abruptly curtailed.

He nodded to her without a flicker of responsive warmth in his enigmatic eyes, and she felt snubbed. Smarting, she thrust through the swing doors of the health centre.

It was humiliating to be regarded as some kind of a threat by a man who enjoyed affairs with a variety of other women, if his own admission and the rumours about him were true!

Patsy was on duty in Reception. 'Don't forget that this afternoon it's your turn for the mums and the new contributions to the population explosion,' she reminded Laurie, running a finger down the list of names in the appointment book. 'Gavin Hunter? Yes. I've found you—just take a seat and wait for Doctor to call your name over the intercom, Gavin.' She smiled at the teenager, then turned to Laurie. 'I'll take the children to Borrowby to see the horses, shall I? Nicky and Giles will give us tea. . .'

She had friends outside the town who owned a stud farm and she had often taken Kay and Jamie there in the past.

'You're a friend,' Laurie told her gratefully. 'I was just wondering if I dared to ask you to have them again!'

'How's Marcus?' asked Patsy.

'Really rather ill, I'm afraid.'

'Poor lamb! So it could be some time before things are back to normal?'

Laurie smiled wryly. 'I'm beginning to believe that things are never normal at Umber House!'

Patsy chuckled. 'It's certainly never dull!'

CHAPTER NINE

ON AN impulse, Laurie took the amiable receptionist up on an earlier suggestion of a night out. 'How about this evening? It won't hurt Judd or Edward to babysit for once,' she said firmly.

'Tonight? Yes, why not? Sounds fun. We'll make a night of it. A film, a meal and a late-night disco at that new place—and I might even meet Mr Right!'

'I didn't know you were still looking,' Laurie ventured, never quite sure of the way things were between Patsy and Judd. They were close, and she suspected that they dated regularly. On the nights that he didn't sleep in his own bed, he might well be in Patsy's, she thought heavily.

'I'm not,' said Patsy. 'I've decided to settle for Mr Almost Right when he shows his face. A girl in my position can't expect miracles. The only men who want to date me are divorced with kids needing a new mum. You'd be surprised at the propositions I get—none of them romantic!' Her smile was cynical. 'Once men married mother-substitutes. Nowadays, the only men I meet seem to want a wife substitute!'

Laurie wondered if she included Judd in that scathing stricture. But it seemed unlikely that he had any desire to marry again—or that Patsy would turn him down if he had, she thought shrewdly.

'How about you?' she asked gently. 'Are you so sure you aren't looking for a father for Kay?'

Patsy grinned. 'Well, of course I am! A handsome six-footer with a bulging wallet who's crazy about animals. That way, both Kay and I will be suited.' Flippancy was her protection against further hurt, concealing a very real loneliness and anxiety about the future. 'Seven-thirty, then?' She reached for the buzzing telephone. 'We'll paint the town red!'

That wasn't quite what she had in mind, Laurie thought wryly as she emerged into the sunshine of the early afternoon. But maybe it was just what she needed to quell the persistent hankering for Judd.

She blinked in surprise to find him pacing up and down between her car and his own, apparently waiting for her to emerge.

'There you are,' he said impatiently 'I'm going over to Wynne House and thought you'd like to come with me and say hello to an old friend.'

'An old friend?' echoed Laurie, puzzled

'Alexander Arbuthnot Mackenzie,' Judd reminded her with a smile that was meant to atone for his recent coolness. After all, it wasn't her fault that he was so wary of yielding to the emotions she inspired in him.

She had almost forgotten the elderly Scotsman. 'Oh, of course. Yes, I'd like to see him,' she agreed. 'But I thought he'd be off on his travels as soon as he left hospital.'

Slipping her car keys into her pocket, she accompanied him into the low, purpose-built extension to the health centre that housed a number of short-stay wards. Admission of disabled or elderly patients provided a welcome respite for carers or convalescence and rehabilitation after illness, accident or surgery.

It was a fairly new concept in community care that had been well received by local GPs and their patients. A bright, cheerful building, surrounded by greenery and gardens, it maintained regular liaison between nurses, physiotherapists, hospital and practice physicians and the social service. Laurie found it impressive.

'I felt he'd benefit from a week or so here,' Judd explained. 'He isn't strong enough to go back on the road, and I've arranged for him to be assessed with a view to a place at Appletree Lodge or Glendale.' He named two of the local council homes for the elderly.

'He'll hate it,' Laurie prophesied, recalling the old man's crusty temperament and stong streak of independence.

'I'm not so sure. He fretted and fumed when he came here, but he's settled down now and enjoying the attention and the security. He's eighty, Laurie. A permanent roof over his head, regular meals and some congenial company might be just what he wants and doesn't know how to go about getting. That accident might have been a blessing in disguise for the poor old devil.'

More evidence of his quiet caring and concern for people and his practical approach to solving their problems, Laurie thought warmly. He was an excellent GP, dedicated to his patients and their variety of needs. Yet he still found time for Jamie, his many friends and a number of non-professional pursuits.

They could spend only a short time with Mr Mackenzie, but he seemed to appreciate their visit. Shaven, sparse grey hair cut and styled by the visiting barber, more flesh on his elderly bones than formerly, he was much improved on the ragged tramp that Judd and Laurie had rescued from a ditch.

She was pleased to have seen him, and said so as they walked back to their respective cars. Judd had a busy afternoon before him, and she had to take home the groceries, make some preparations for the evening meal and then return for the mother and baby clinic.

'He's a wily old bird. You won't clip his wings,' she added confidently. 'I don't think you'll get him into local authority housing of any description.'

'We'll see. He has a shadow on one lung and his liver's in pretty poor condition. I'm not prepared to sit back and let him ride off into the sunset on that battered old bike to die on some lonely road. I've talked sense into more stubborn heads than that one, in my time.'

Laurie didn't doubt it, having seen Judd in action more than once when a patient was refusing referral to a hospital or rejecting the treatment he recommended. 'Well, I wish you luck!'

Hands plunged deep into trouser pockets to keep from reaching out for her, Judd absently jingled coins, an unconscious habit at moments of uncertainty. He looked down at her thoughtfully as she paused beside her small car.

Slim and pretty in mint-green trousers and skimpy blouse, smudged shadows beneath dark blue eyes with their velvet sweep of long, thick lashes and unruly curls hastily tied back with a ribbon, she looked absurdly youthful and touchingly vulnerable, catching at his unwilling heart.

She was all soft, sweet temptation that insidiously eroded his deep-seated resolve never to love again, and, with an effort, he steeled his softening resistance.

But he couldn't keep concern from his deep voice as he said abruptly, 'You're tired, Laurie. You're doing too much.'

She was heartened that he'd noticed that she rushed hither and thither, cramming twenty-five hours into each busy day. 'Do I have a choice?' she countered lightly. 'Someone has to take care of things at home.'

Home. It was the first time she had consciously connected the word with her new abode, and the trite old tag about home being where the heart lay sprang to mind. Briefly, she wondered if her heart had slipped its leash in spite of her determination to hold on to it.

Judd frowned. 'Of course you have a choice! You came here as a doctor, not a domestic,' he said impatiently. 'You shouldn't be wasting your time on the trivia of housework and child care. *I* don't expect you to cook and clean and run around after Jamie and Jenefer.'

Laurie hastened to correct the obvious impression that she resented the chores that had been thrust on her. Deep down she was mother and homemaker as much as physician, and there was a satisfaction of a different kind in all that she was doing for the children.

'I'd prefer to do more in the practice, naturally. But that isn't possible while Marcus is so ill and Serene has to stay close to him. In the meantime, I put in a few hours at the surgery each day, and as for the rest—well, the house won't run itself, and I really enjoy my time with the children.'

'You shouldn't be carrying all the burden, nevertheless. Edward could do more,' Judd said with a hint of censure. 'And I'll see to it that Jamie is less of a problem.'

'But Jamie *isn't* a problem,' Laurie protested, guarding the precious hours she shared with the little boy. Jamie was a comforting link with a man who seemed determined to keep her at a distance in spite of her growing bond with his son.

It was apparently all right for her to devote time to Jamie, to take care of Jamie, to become more and more important to Jamie, but his father made it painfully plain that there was no place for her in *his* heart or *his* life. And Laurie was too proud and too fearful to show by word or glance or gesture that it was too late to keep him out of *her* heart.

'I'm sure he must be a nuisance to you at times,' he insisted, convinced that only a loving mother could tolerate the incessant demands made upon her by a small boy, both by day and night.

'No. I love him,' Laurie said simply.

I love him, her heart echoed in wonder, meaning Jamie's father, as she looked into the doubting, brilliantly blue eyes of a man who had put up the barriers as soon as he felt threatened by her presence in Umber.

Panicked by the revelation, she fumbled with car keys and a suddenly awkward lock, afraid that his piercing, too perceptive gaze would recognise the betrayal in her glowing face and visibly trembling fingers.

How could she stay in Umber and see Judd every day without showing her sudden, overwhelming love for him? And how could she avoid the inevitable heartache that accompanied the folly of caring for a man who had no heart to give?

'I believe you really mean that,' Judd said with quiet gratitude.

The golden glory of his smile engulfed Laurie, quickening her to another spasm of newly recognised love and need. 'I do.' How easy to admit her love for the boy, how utterly impossible to confess that she had lost her heart to the man?

He smiled down at her. 'He's a different child since you came, much happier, more confident, doing better at school, having fewer bad dreams. If only Marla had been half as caring. . .' He broke off, his mouth hardening. 'Well, we won't talk about Marla,' he decided grimly, knowing he couldn't compare the selfish, irresponsible woman he had married with this warm-hearted girl who had enchanted Jamie and come close to enchanting him too, with her laughing eyes and lovely smile and tender, loving concern.

'Do you ever hear from her?' Tentatively but deliberately, Laurie probed the wound, feeling that maybe he *should* talk about Marla, exorcise the memory and the pain and the love he still felt, start the slow process of a healing that might one day enable him to forget that his ex-wife was essential to his happiness.

Judd shrugged. 'Jamie's birthday. At Christmas. The occasional postcard from exotic parts. She sends presents. Jamie put the last one in the dustbin without opening it. Nothing to do with me,' he added quickly as her eyes widened. 'I try not to influence him. But he feels these things more deeply than we realise, I think.'

Laurie agreed, thinking about the bad dreams and their probable cause. She didn't need a degree in child pyschology to recognise that Jamie badly missed his mother and needed constant assurances that he wasn't responsible in some way for her early departure from his life. He might be too young to remember Marla, but there was no doubt in Laurie's mind that he sensed the void caused by her desertion.

He must sense his father's loneliness and longing too. Just as she did, loving him, aching for him, eager to ease his pain and bitterness in any way she could. Wrenched by compassion as well as her own innermost needs, she wanted to put her arms about him and give him ease and forgetfulness with her lips and body. Hurt ripped through her as she remembered that he didn't seem to want her as friend, lover or anything else.

'Doesn't she ever want to see him?' It seemed inconceivable to Laurie that a mother could be so unloving, so indifferent.

'Australia's a long way away,' Judd said flatly, and got into his car, closing the door with a snap of finality.

A long way away. Laurie silently echoed the words as he drove off. The other side of the world. But Marla was right here in Umber, a constant and very vivid presence in all their lives, an insurmountable obstacle to the fulfilment of a wildly impossible dream. Marla might be living in Australia, but it was obvious that she still resided in Judd's heart and mind, denying the right of even the smallest seed of affection for someone else to germinate and grow and drive her out.

Judd clung to a past that cast its dark shadow to blot out all hope of a brighter, happier future, and he seemed to want to go on loving Marla, hopelessly, pointlessly, fantasising that one day she would be back, repentant and regretful and ready to pick up the threads of their marriage.

Laurie sighed. Once she had believed that caring for someone was all joy and delight and bright hope of happiness. For the second time, she had discovered that it could hurt. And this time it promised to hurt for the rest of her life.

She was late home that evening, for her last patient at the mother and baby clinic was a tearful young mother who couldn't cope with an incessantly crying baby.

Suspecting a medical cause for the colic and sickness and sleepless nights, Laurie carried out a careful examination and referred the baby to hospital for urgent surgical investigation of a probable intestinal blockage.

Learning that the baby's mother had no husband, no money and no family back-up, she had then driven them both to the Northwood General in her own car.

'You've all the makings of a first-class GP,' declared Judd, having heard the story from Patsy before Laurie finally arrived at Umber House. 'You really care about patients and don't mind giving up your own time to them.' He sent her an approving smile, then turned back to the cooker.

Domesticity sat lightly on his broad shoulders. In shirt-sleeves and with a blue-striped apron tied about his waist, he was potently masculine and very attractive.

To hide the glow in her face at the rare praise, Laurie bent to look at Jamie's drawing of a horse as he sat at the kitchen table and dropped a kiss on his hair as she admired his efforts.

A self-important Jenefer helped Judd, slicing tomatoes and washing lettuce, while an excited Kay raced about the garden, pursued by a barking dog. Patsy had left her daughter with Judd while she went home to change for the evening.

'She couldn't get a baby-sitter at short notice, so I said Kay can sleep here tonight,' he explained. 'So there's no reason why you two girls shouldn't stay out all night if you like.' He grinned. 'Paint the town red.'

He echoed Patsy's light words, and Laurie felt a twisting envy of their friendship. But she reminded herself sensibly that they had known each other long before she came on the scene and had much in common that she was inevitably excluded from sharing.

Such as a broken marriage and a child with only one parent. . .

'Oh, we will,' she assured him brightly. 'As long as you really don't mind. . .'

'Not at all. Kay's going to sleep with Jenefer, and they're both so excited that I'll probably be in and out of the room a dozen times before they finally settle down. Eh, Jenny?' He tweaked one of the little girl's shining braids and she beamed at him. 'Part of the fun of childhood, isn't it? Only children miss out on a lot.'

Laurie glanced from beneath the thick fan of her dark lashes. 'Then perhaps you should do something about providing Jamie with a brother or sister. I'm sure there must be one or two women who'd oblige!' It was a teasing tilt at his popularity with some of the female patients who haunted the surgery. Emboldened by the warmly domestic atmosphere and his affable mood, she tossed the words at him with a smiling challenge in her sapphire eyes.

'One or two,' he agreed smoothly, sharing the joke. 'But I doubt if any of them would meet with Jamie's approval. He's very hard to please.'

As his artistic son glanced up from the careful, clever sketch of galloping horses that was inspired by the afternoon's visit to the stud farm, Judd silenced him with a warning frown, aware that Jamie was about to suggest for the umpteenth time that his father should marry Dr Laurie.

The thought had lurked in the deepest recesses of his own mind ever since he had met her, along with the growing desire that was centred as much on a need for her tender, unselfish love as for her beautiful body.

He had no intention of admitting it, however.

'He'd probably say yes to Patsy.' The unthinking words were out before Laurie could check them, tinged with a shameful jealousy. 'He's very fond of her,' she added lamely as Judd raised an astonished eyebrow.

He wondered who or what had given her the idea that Patsy was a likely candidate for his heart. 'Ah, but would Patsy say yes to me?' he countered, smiling. 'And if she did, would Jamie ever forgive me for turning Kay into his little sister?'

The light words made Laurie laugh, for everyone knew Jamie's feeling about Kay. Like all little boys, he loathed being kissed and fussed over and followed about by the purposeful little girl who declared that she meant to marry him one day. Jamie yukked and shuddered and pushed her away, to no avail, and complained that the boys at school teased him about his blonde girlfriend. Whenever he ran to her attic sanctuary in search of Laurie, usually followed by a panting, tail-wagging Angelo who had no respect for her privacy or her possessions, it was usually to escape the torment of Kay's persistent pursuit.

He was very like Judd in the way he put up barriers to protect himself from feminine wiles he distrusted because of his mother's defection. But Laurie was painfully aware that Judd wasn't likely to follow his son's example and turn to her for comfort of any kind.

'I must go and change,' she said, a little reluctant to leave the cosy domestic scene. 'If you're sure you can manage. . .?'

'I can manage,' Judd assured her firmly, lowering the heat beneath the simmering, savoury-smelling pan of meat and sauces and herbs. 'Off you go and get ready for your evening, Cinderella.'

She smiled. 'That smells good.' She lingered, wistful, regretting the impulse that had led to the arrangement with Patsy. She could have enjoyed helping Judd with dinner, sitting around the big table with him and the children, fooling around with him while they washed up and then snuggling up on the sofa to watch television or listen to music when the children were in bed.

But such delights were reserved for couples, she reminded herself ruefully. Single girls like herself were condemned to evenings spent in wine bars and discos, fighting off amorous men.

'I'm a man of many talents. Doctoring, cooking, baby-minding—you name it and I've probably done it.' His blue eyes kindled with humour. 'You'll miss a rare culinary treat. Ask Angelo!' He flicked a teacloth at the boisterous dog as he bounded into the kitchen from the garden door, almost knocking Jenefer off her feet and scattering Jamie's array of colouring pencils with a brush of his tail. 'He's cleared the plates lots of times when no one else would touch my dish of the day!'

Jenefer giggled and Jamie grinned, and Laurie laughed aloud, gladdened by his lightness of heart and daring to believe that, like Jamie, Judd was happier since she had come to Umber.

'I know you're joking,' she reproached, smiling at him.

She was lovely, amusement animating her delicate features and sparkling in her sapphire eyes, mere prettiness transformed to such glowing beauty that Judd's heart contracted and his body leaped with longing. That beauty came from within, he knew, a pure and precious glow of goodness and warmth and honesty, making her a woman that any man would want—and he wanted her very much indeed.

But a lingering mistrust and a fierce concern for his son's future overshadowed the feelings that Laurie inspired. For how could he be sure that she wouldn't hurt and disappoint and desert them, just as Marla had done?

He drew back instinctively from the threshold of loving and the pain he knew it could bring.

'Yes, I'm joking,' he agreed heavily. 'I'm an excellent cook, in fact. I'm good at most things, but an absolute failure as a husband.' The humour had vanished from his eyes and voice. Grim-faced, a brooding light in narrowed eyes, he added, 'Which explains why I've no desire to marry again.'

'Judd, I'm sorry. . .' Laurie didn't know why she apologised, unless it was because she felt she had raked up best-buried hurts with her teasing.

She looked at his speaking back as he stirred the goulash, longing to put comforting arms about him but inhibited by the presence of the children, who looked bewildered and slightly alarmed by the sudden change of tone.

The atmosphere had turned tense, fraught with Judd's anger and her own dismay, and Laurie wisely went quietly from the room.

CHAPTER TEN

LATER, she confided in Patsy, saying nothing about her own mixed-up emotions but confessing that she felt she had unwittingly wounded Judd.

'It *is* strange that he hasn't married again, don't you think?' she went on tentatively. 'He cares so much about Jamie, and that's one little boy who really needs a mother, even if she isn't his own.' She hesitated. 'I suppose Marla was very special?'

'I never met her,' said Patsy, 'but everyone says she wasn't cut out for the wife and mother role. Do you remember the series of TV ads for Fantasy—my favourite perfume, actually!—featuring the gorgeous girl who dreams about an unattainable man. . .a famous actor or pop star. . .and meets him the day she starts to wear Fantasy? Well, Marla was that girl.'

Laurie vaguely recalled the publicity generated by the successful commercials and the readiness of some very famous men to appear in them, but she had been busy with medical studies at the time and seldom watched television. The Fantasy Girl had been much talked about, much photographed, much sought after for a time, and then, like so many others, had faded from the advertising scene. In Marla's case, apparently leaving husband and infant son to begin a new life in Australia.

'Sounds glamorous.' She marvelled that she'd foolishly supposed she could tempt the heart or the body of a man who had once been married to the Fantasy Girl. It was no competition!

'The last thing a GP needs is a glamorous wife who's away for weeks at a time with her job and is dissatisfied when she's home because she doesn't understand the demands of his job,' Patsy pointed out sagely. 'She was just starting out as a model when they married, and I expect Judd was proud of her, pleased when she got work, but thought it would all fizzle out when Jamie was born. Having him must have given her a special glow, because it was a mother-and-baby ad that brought her to the public eye. Suddenly she was the face of the year and everyone wanted her, and, of course, it was only a matter of time before she met someone she preferred to Judd.' She shook her head. 'Frankly, I don't know how she *could*!'

Laurie drank some coffee. 'He is nice,' she agreed cautiously.

'Every woman's dream!'

'Including yours?' Laurie managed to make it sound teasing rather than probing.

Patsy blew a smoke ring and watched it spiral and slowly dissolve before she answered. 'I thought we had something going at one time. But I'm not the kind to waste my dreams on the unattainable, and I honestly don't believe the woman exists who can take Marla's place in Judd's life.'

Laurie's heart sank at the confirmation of her own

fears. 'And he still thinks she might come back one day, I suppose?'

'Maybe she will. She's unpredictable, apparently. She might even be missing Jamie. It's ironic that she made her name promoting a baby product and then abandoned her own infant at the first opportunity, don't you think?'

'I think it's sad that she's missed his baby years, the most precious years. Perhaps she felt he'd be better with Judd than living an unpredictable and unsettled life with a model mother,' Laurie suggested generously.

'You're too charitable!' Patsy snorted. '*I* think she's just plain bloody selfish, and it beats me that someone as attractive and as clever as Judd can be so stupidly besotted with such a woman!'

So she *had* tried her luck with Judd and failed! Laurie smiled sympathetically. 'It's called love, Patsy,' she said gently.

And she knew all about love, she thought with a pang. It obsessed, consumed, dictated almost every waking thought as well as her dreams. But it wouldn't do to let Patsy guess how she felt about Judd. She didn't trust her matchmaking instincts!

As a result of the new drug, Marcus seemed to improve, but Serene was still spending more of her time at the hospital than Umber House, and in the circumstances Laurie felt she could scarcely complain. She had managed to work out a routine that seemed to suit everyone pretty well.

It allowed her to fill the gap in the practice left by Edward's frequent absences as he continued to support Serene far more than anyone could expect from a mere friend of the family. It was a dire suspicion, but Laurie was beginning to wonder if his deep anxiety about Marcus had a more significant foundation.

Was he, in fact, the baby's father?

She didn't like to mention her suspicion to Judd or Patsy, and certainly not to her cousin, but Edward himself confirmed that she had hit on the truth when she met him on his return from the Northwood General one afternoon.

He was looking anxious, and she delayed her departure for the surgery to find out what was wrong.

'Is it Marcus?' she asked gently.

'He isn't well again, Laurie. Curtis can't give any good reason for it, but he's rapidly going downhill, to my eyes. Serene is staying with him, but I can't sit there and watch my boy die. . .' His voice broke.

Laurie instantly put her arms around him. 'He isn't going to die, Edward,' she assured him stoutly. 'Michael Curtis is a very good doctor, and I'm sure he's doing all the right things for Marcus.'

She didn't show any surprise or shock. She supposed she had known from the beginning that Edward had a vested interest in Serene Lipski and one at least of her two children.

'This isn't like you,' she continued, rallying him, hugging him. 'You always look on the bright side!'

'It isn't easy when it's your own flesh and blood hooked up to a life support system!' He drew away to look into her uncondemning eyes. 'You guessed, didn't you?'

'It occurred to me that he might be yours—yes, Edward,' she admitted quietly.

'Well, he is. Serene was divorcing Paul. She couldn't stand his gambling any more. I believe I told you she didn't know about his debts. In fact, she didn't know the *extent* of them, but he'd mortgaged the house and sold every asset he could put his hands on to finance his stupid obsession,' he said bitterly. 'He led her the hell of a life, and she was too loyal for years to admit it to anyone.'

'Did he know that Marcus. . .?' Laurie broke off, reluctant to put it into actual words. She had seen too much of the world and its ways at Hartlake to be shocked, but she was a little dismayed and doing her best not to be disapproving; it was the last thing she would have expected from her circumspect cousin. Which proved how little anyone ever really knew about other people!

'Oh, he knew. Gave us his blessing, to tell the truth. It hit him hard, though. Men like Paul never imagine that their wives or families are suffering through their thoughtless behaviour, do they?'

'But he wasn't contesting the divorce?'

'No—just looking for as many delaying factors as he could. I think he wanted the baby to carry his name. He always wanted an heir—not that he had much to leave even a proxy son in the end.'

'Serene must have had a really bad time of it in the past year,' Laurie suggested with her instinctive compassion. No wonder she had felt that the woman's apparent composure was just a façade! She had apparently spent years putting on a front for the world.

'And Paul finally realised what he'd done to her, I think. Sometimes I wonder if his death was really due to an accident or if he'd deliberately stopped on the motorway and waited for something to hit him. A way out of all his problems, perhaps.'

'You aren't serious!' gasped Laurie.

He nodded. 'The final grand gesture—it would be in character. But don't ever say anything of the kind to Serene, will you? She blames herself enough as it is—says it would never have happened if she hadn't had Marcus. He was on his way to see her and the baby, you see. He took an interest, whereas another man might have washed his hands of us all.' Edward slumped into a chair and took the drink that Laurie had poured for him. 'I'm sorry to burden you with all this, Laurie. . .'

She shrugged off the unnecessary apology. 'Do you and Serene mean to get married eventually?'

'At the moment, it's a taboo subject. I told you, she blames herself for what happened to Paul. She feels we should have done things in the right order—waited for the divorce to go through, got married and then had Marcus. It's going to take a little time to persuade her to marry me, I'm afraid.'

'At least you managed to persuade her to sell up and move in with you,' she comforted. 'I know you aren't actually *together*. . .'

Edward smiled at her diplomatic choice of words. 'That's going to take time too. But I'm a patient man. I loved Serene long before she met Paul and I know things will work out for us in time. Just now, my main concern is for Marcus.'

'Very naturally.' Laurie glanced at her watch. 'I have to go,' she said regretfully. 'Afternoon surgery.' She paused on her way to the door. 'I won't repeat any of this, of course.'

'Judd knows the score.'

'Oh. . .oh, yes, I suppose he would.' She stifled a faint hurt that Edward had confided in his partner rather than the cousin, who had always considered herself to be a good friend.

'I needed his permission for Serene to move in,' Edward explained.

Permission seemed an odd word for him to use. After all, Umber House belonged to Edward, and he could surely invite anyone he wished to live beneath his roof.

But perhaps his arrangement with Judd included sharing the house.

'Why should he object?' queried Laurie. 'You both need someone to take care of the domestic side—Judd more than you, with Jamie to consider!'

'How are you getting on with him these days?' Edward asked her. 'I felt you didn't like him too much at first.'

'It's working out.'

'He has a lot on his mind at the moment, so make allowances for him, won't you?'

'Any particular problem?' She tried not to seem too enquiring.

'Nothing medical. He's having a fight with Marla

over custody of Jamie. It seems he didn't apply for it at the time of the divorce and she was happy to leave the boy with him. Now he's trying to make it legal, and she's objecting. He has to go to London for the court hearing next week, and it seems that Marla has threatened to appear with a counter-claim.'

'Can she do that after so long?' queried Laurie.

'She's the boy's mother. She still has some rights, apparently.'

No wonder Judd had been so distant, so preoccupied in the last few weeks—and no wonder he was disinclined to find her as attractive as she found him, Laurie thought as she drove her small gold Fiesta to the health centre. He had much more on his mind than a possible relationship with a new woman. He was still trying to solve some of the problems caused by the previous one!

He must be fearful of losing Jamie, although it seemed unlikely to Laurie's logical mind that any court would grant custody to his long-absent mother. It seemed a particularly spiteful act by the unknown Marla, who had apparently only decided she wanted her son when she learned that Judd was applying for legal custody after six years of being wholly responsible for his welfare and his upbringing.

It was hard to keep her mind on the medical problems of her patients that afternoon. She listened to chests and took pulses and blood-pressures and inspected eyes and ears and mouths, wrote prescriptions and gave advice and listened patiently to complaints and questions like the good GP she was rapidly becoming, but in her mind's eye she saw Judd arguing his case before a judge who didn't know the great love he bore for Jamie or how caring and conscientious a father he had been all through the years of making up for a missing mother.

She was sounding a chest for the umpteenth time that day when the consulting-room door opened and Sister Beavis looked in. Laurie observed her entry, but couldn't hear what she was saying for the ear-pieces and the irregular thump and boom of a valvular disfunction.

She removed the sounding-piece of the stethoscope from Mr Morrison's chest and glanced enquiringly at the practice sister.

'Can you spare a moment, Doctor? I'm sorry to call you away, but I'm sure Mr Morrison won't mind. . .'

Sister's tone was calm, but the urgency of her expression told Laurie that she was needed to deal with an emergency. She rose to her feet and followed Sister Beavis from the room with an apologetic murmur for the patient.

'What's the problem?' she asked as soon as the door was closed on Mr Morrison.

'It's Mrs Morrison. I didn't want to alarm the poor man just yet, but she seems to be having a heart attack. She was waiting for her husband in Reception when Lesley noticed that she seemed to be in some distress. I've managed to get her into an examination-room. . .' Sister opened a nearby door.

Mrs Morrison looked ashen, and the blue tinge to her lips told Laurie that the woman had a chronic cardiac condition. She was obviously still having chest pains and her breathing was rapid and laboured. After a quick examination to confirm the obvious, Laurie gave her an injection of coramine to ease the cramping pains and ordered an ambulance to transfer the patient to the Northwood General for emergency admission to the cardiac unit.

She then had the unenviable task of telling Mr Morrison that his wife was being taken to hospital. He didn't seem surprised.

'I told her she needed to see the doctor more than I did,' he said bluntly. 'She's not been well for a day or two, but there's no telling you women anything. "I'm all right," she says. "It's you I'm worried about." Wouldn't even trust me to get to the surgery without her, daft 'aporth—and a fat lot of good that's done her! I suppose I'd best go in the ambulance with her, Doctor?'

'I think she'd like you to go along,' Laurie said, startled that there was any doubt in the matter. But they were both old and perhaps he felt unable to cope with the situation. Considering that he had just learned that he had a heart problem of his own, albeit minor compared to his wife's, Laurie was thankful that her elderly patient had taken the bad news so well.

A few days later she heard that Mrs Morrison had died, and she made a mental note to go and see Mr Morrison and offer condolences as well as practical help. He was a product of his generation who had probably never cooked a meal or laundered for himself, and he would be a lost soul after nearly fifty years of having his wife to look after him.

The business of cooking and cleaning was still very much a woman's work, in spite of all the strides made towards liberating her sex from such mundane matters, Laurie thought drily, as she made beds and dusted the following morning before making her way to the surgery to put in a couple of hours.

As she straightened the curtain at Jamie's bedroom window, she caught a glimpse of vivid scarlet in the drive, halfway between house and gate. Her hand froze. Someone, a woman, stood beneath the trees, half hidden.

Laurie thought she recognised the bright colour and the fashionable elegance of her suit and matching hat. It was surely the same woman who had been at the school gate that morning when she dropped Jamie and Jenefer and who had looked so hard and so strangely at her that she clearly recalled the incident. Surely she had also been in the surgery car park when she was supervising the transfer to an ambulance of an asthmatic eight-year-old who had suffered a severe attack in her consulting-room the previous afternoon?

A patient, obviously. But what was she doing here? It was a practice rule that patients were only seen at the surgery or in their own homes.

Puzzled, Laurie turned from the window and gave a last, tidying tug to the duvet and trundled the Hoover from the room. Perhaps the woman had seen the advertisement on the surgery notice-board for someone to help with the housework and shopping and had decided to take a look at Umber House before she applied for the job. She didn't look a likely candidate, but it was impossible to judge by appearances, Laurie reminded herself with a wry smile. After all, who would immediately recognise *her* as a doctor if they saw her plugging the Hoover into the socket in Judd's room?

The airing bed still bore the impress of his head on the pillow. Fondly, rather foolishly, she laid her hand on the place where his sleeping head had rested. Dear Judd, so very dear—and so distant these days that she felt she would never again know the sweet intoxication of his kiss.

She looked around the room with its few signs of his occupation. Like Judd himself, it gave away very little. No photographs, not even of Jamie. A set of silver-backed brushes with his engraved initials, the aroma of aftershave, a pair of leather slippers that he seldom found time to wear, an expensive, heavy silk dressing-gown that Laurie daringly held to her face so that she could breathe the lingering male scent of his body.

With heady desire in her veins, she allowed herself to fantasise about sinking into the big double bed with him, arms about each other, seeking to touch and kiss and hold in a frenzy of mutual longing, bodies intertwining as they pursued the enchantment and the ecstacy of passionate lovemaking.

Eyes closed, Laurie hugged his robe and swayed in a delicious dream of him, an exciting and dangerously erotic dream that was rudely shattered as Judd strode into the room.

He stopped short. Face flaming, she dropped his

dressing-gown as if it was molten lead, guilt tingling from head to toe along with the flame of wanton desire.

'Oh, Judd! I didn't know you were in! I was just. . .tidying up,' she said lamely.

Judd retrieved his dressing-gown from the floor and tossed it on the bed, aware that he had startled her but puzzled by her embarrassment. The stain of the hot blush swept from hairline to slender throat and the swell of tempting breasts at the scoop neckline of her blouse.

His pulses leaped with the longing to follow the trail of that betraying blush with warm lips, her presence in his very private domain setting up such a storm of desire that he almost swept her into his arms and stifled any protest she might make with the passion in his embrace.

'I need Mrs Flanagan's notes and stupidly left them behind this morning.' He took a folder from the drawer beside the bed. 'I wrote them up last night in bed. I'm seeing someone from the social services about her today.'

'Do I know Mrs Flanagan?' Laurie seized on the impersonal discussion of a patient to cover her confusion while her flurrying heart slowed and the heat in her face died down.

'Little old lady with arthritis. Patchett Lane. She's too old and frail to cope on her own and too stubborn to go into community care.' He smiled wryly. 'She says she can't abide old folk, and such places are full of them! But now that she's ninety-two and can't see so well, she admits to needing a little help,'

'I hope I'm as independent at that age!'

Judd's eyes warmed as they rested on her delicately pretty face and the slender shape of her young body in the colourful skirt and blouse, the warm autumn shades of yellows and greens and soft honey enhancing her dark, captivating beauty.

'Unlike Mrs Flanagan, you'll probably have family to care about you—children and grandchildren, no doubt—and won't need to call on the social services.'

It was a light-hearted assurance, but something twisted painfully in his breast at the thought that one day Laurie would find someone else to love, would marry and go away from Judd and Jamie and Umber. He had made the same mistake as his innocently unaware son, after all. He had given his heart to this girl.

'I don't expect to marry,' Laurie said stiffly. He was all she wanted, with all her heart. Judd—and Jamie. But it seemed an impossible dream. 'So there won't *be* children, or grandchildren.'

Judd was wrenched with compassion. Doctors could heal most things, but not broken hearts, and even the willing gift of his love might not comfort the lovely Laurie for the dismay and disappointment of a lost love.

He smiled at her, believing he knew and understood her pain, just a breath away from touching her, taking her into arms that craved to contain her.

'Wounds heal, Laurie,' he told her gently.

CHAPTER ELEVEN

LAURIE looked at him with doubt in her sapphire eyes. 'Do they?' She was sure that *his* hurts were still raw and angry and might never respond to the soothing balm of another woman's embrace. But oh, how her heart trembled with love for him and the ardent longing to make up to him for all the pain of the past! On a sigh she couldn't help, she looked away before he read too much into her steady gaze.

'I know you don't think so now, but time *does* help,' Judd promised, recalling his own despair and its eventual lightening, and what a difference it had made to his life and his future when Laurie walked into it. He was thankful now that he had taken steps to sever the last link with Marla by claiming legal custody of Jamie, long after he should have done so.

Hearing the kindly concern in his deep voice, Laurie knew he hopelessly misinterpreted her feelings, and she longed to put him right. But it wouldn't help for him to know that she loved him when he was a million light-years away from caring anything for her. In fact, it would make matters worse. For she couldn't bear his sympathy and his concerned regret that he had no heart to offer her in return.

'My feelings won't change,' she said. 'Ever.' And it didn't seem important to add that she wasn't thinking of Cris as she spoke the words with their fierce ring of truth.

'Well. . .' Judd was at a loss. He ought to approve the lasting power of her love and the strength of her loyalty, even for a lost cause, but he was only conscious of engulfing dismay. He managed a wry smile. 'For people like us, there's always work, I suppose.' How thankful he had been for his profession and its demands in the past. But he hadn't anticipated the need to don its armour to shield his disappointed heart all over again.

'Yes—and that reminds me! I think we may have a response to our appeal for a cleaning lady.' Laurie seized on a valid reason to change the subject. 'There was someone hanging about outside just now who seemed very interested in the house. Did you see her as you drove in?'

'I don't think so.'

'Thirtyish, attractive, very smart. I've seen her in the village *and* at the surgery, I think. Not the kind I'd expect to want the job, frankly, but maybe she needs to supplement her income and feels there's a cachet in working for a houseful of doctors.'

Judd frowned. 'Willing to flick a duster and arrange a few flowers and do a little light shopping but not much else? I know the kind. Not at all suitable.'

'And you recognise the right kind for domestic work at a glance, don't you?' Laurie couldn't resist teasing him.

'I suppose you'll never let me forget our first encounter!' he laughed.

'Well, it wasn't exactly romantic!' Her face flamed as she realised the betrayal of the impulsive reproach. 'Not that it should have been, of course,' she blundered on, making things worse, the blush deepening and spreading as she saw the amusement in his speaking eyes. 'I mean. . .I should have said *flattering*.'

'I did rather dent your ego,' he admitted, smiling, 'Six years to qualify as a doctor and I assumed you were just another woman!' The remarkably blue eyes danced.

There was an unconscious coquetry in Laurie's eyes as she looked up at him, a provocative smile lifting her lips. 'Oh, I'm a woman as well, Judd,' she said softly.

Judd stiffened. As if he needed the reminder—or could resist such an invitation! Wanting her had become a constant ache, a growing need, a tension that severely strained his self-control, so much so that he had feared there must sooner or later be an explosion of emotion, culminating either in the conquest he so desired or in a complete rout.

Now, she leaned towards him, tempting him, the Eve that lurked in every woman smiling at him through Laurie's beautiful eyes; and, like Adam, he fell.

He kissed her, quickly, a little roughly, snatching at the sweetness of that tremulous mouth. With passion storming his senses, an uncontrollable tumult of desire flooding him to sweep away all caution, he was suddenly urgent for the fusion and the release to be found in her arms. Putting gentle but insistent hands on her slim shoulders, he drew her slowly, inexorably closer.

As she remembered the brusque rebuff he had dealt her as well as the offhand attitude that had hurt so much, pride should have kept Laurie from sliding her arms about his neck and giving her lips on a soft, sighing surrender. But she was beyond pride. Love was dictating her responses, and nothing mattered but the urgency of his mouth, the hard thrust of his powerful body, the growing need in herself to match the rising, forceful passion and experience for the first time the real meaning of a man's all-consuming embrace.

They kissed and clung and kissed again, like lovers who couldn't get enough of each other after long separation. His mouth warmed and wooed her response with sweet, sensual kisses, and Laurie wound her arms about him and ploughed her fingers through the thick tangle of his splendid hair and urged him on with throaty murmurs as desire drove out every other consideration.

Judd drew her down to the yielding bed and an embrace that was ardent but inexpressibly tender. There was no thought in Laurie's mind of protest or resistance, for it seemed so right, so natural and entirely inevitable—two hurt and lonely people coming together in mutual, joyous need.

Slowly, reverently, Judd drew off each garment until she was nude and lovely in his arms, rosy from his kisses and an appealing hint of shyness. Cradling the small, soft breasts, he praised each in turn with eyes and lips and gentle caress, and Laurie revelled in her woman's power over a proud, enigmatic man who had finally succumbed with his body if not his heart.

They were breathlessly close to the ultimate intimacy, and there would be no hesitation, no turning back and no regrets on her part. For wasn't this what she had dreamed of and desired for weeks? Wasn't it the heartfelt expression of her love for him? Later, she would face the awesome possibility that she meant no more to a fiercely sensual man after than before she lay in his arms and gave herself gladly for his pleasure and her own.

Judd explored and adored every inch of her body with lips and clever hands, pleasing and teasing and arousing her to near-frantic excitement, kissing her between those subtle, strongly moving caresses with a tenderness and a patience that almost moved her to tears, murmuring endearments she had never expected to hear on his lips and, with the wisdom of Eve, forbore to question.

Desire and delight quivered along every nerve and through every vein as he made skilful, sensitive love to her, and she kissed him back with her heart on her lips, stroking bare, bronzed shoulders and back, powerful, male-scented chest and lean, hard buttocks and thighs with a touch that spoke of love and need and longing.

Thrilled by her warm, womanly response, knowing he wanted to share the rest of his life with her, Judd trailed a tender route from the meltingly-sweet mouth and throbbing pulses in the slender neck to the soft silk of shoulders and breasts, the quiver of youthfully flat belly and the tremble of thighs with seeking, sensuous lips and hands, and felt her body arch and offer itself in fiercely passionate arousal.

Now was the moment, he knew—and she uttered a soft little sound that might have been his name or a sweet sigh of contentment as his equally urgent body slid home. Her arms tightened about him as he paused to savour that most exquisite of delights. He kissed her mouth, the tip of her pretty nose, the closed eyes, and saw the secret Eve's smile that wreathed her lovely face as she welcomed his pleasure in her receptive body.

She was beautiful, beautiful, and he loved her dearly—and said so as he buried his thankful face in the soft, scented tumble of her dark hair.

'I love you, Laurie. . .'

The aching murmur pierced her heart. 'No. . .' She silenced him, first with fingertips and then lips, soothing him with her tender touch of his burnished hair, his strong neck and lean cheek. 'It doesn't matter, Judd.' But it *did*—oh, it *did*! Far more than she ever could or would admit. But he mustn't feel that he had to lie to make her feel better at this supreme moment.

He must know she loved him—and how could she keep it from him when every kiss, every quiver of her virgin body blazoned the truth?

Judd understood. It was too soon.

Gathering Laurie closer, he kissed her, and their bodies began to move together in the slow, sensual rhythm of congress, but Judd had been patient too long and his body soon took masterful charge, quickening and urging and storming her to new heights.

She was swept with him on a rising crescendo of sensation that took them both to the magical, tumultuous peaks of passion and beyond and then slowly, very slowly, stranded them on the breathless shores of after-love.

They held each other for a time, spent and content, silent because lips and bodies had already said it all, thudding hearts gradually calming.

At last Judd stirred, reluctant to release her now they had found the way to a new and very precious intimacy but knowing they couldn't lie forever in each other's arms, much as it might delight him.

He raised on an elbow to look down on her glowing, luminously lovely face. 'Where do we go from here?' he asked softly, knowing what *he* wanted with all his being but anxious not to rush her into anything.

Laurie didn't know what he wanted or expected her to answer, so she took refuge in the mundane. 'You to your meeting with the social services, and me to the surgery!' she said, twisting his lean wrist to look at his watch. 'I promised Edward to put in an hour or two this morning.'

'My meeting began ten minutes ago,' he confessed without regret.

They disentangled slowly, with sighs and soft murmurs and kisses, and it took all Judd's strength of mind to keep from exploring newfound paradise in her willing arms again.

Laurie sat up, brushing the tousle of unruly curls

from her radiant face. 'Doctors have a ready-made excuse for unpunctuality,' she reminded him with laughing eyes. 'Tell them you've been brushing up on your bedside skills!'

He gave a delighted laugh, looking so young, so relaxed and so content that her heart turned over. It was worth everything, even the pain of knowing it was his sensuality rather than any degree of love on his part that had brought them together, to see just that look on his dear face. He was so like Jamie, and she loved them both so much.

She let Judd shower first, for his meeting was more important than her stint at the surgery. She knew Edward would cover for her without question.

He sang in the shower, the deep bass of his pleasant voice booming through the rush of cascading water, and Laurie hugged the intimate insight into the man to her heart.

She didn't know where they went from here, any more than he did, but at least she had a golden memory to treasure, no matter how or why it had come about.

He dressed while she showered, and then there was a special kind of tender loving care in the way he wrapped her around with a thickly luxuriant towel as she stepped from the shower, then dried her with gentle hands as if she were a child rather than the woman who had just delighted him with her secrets.

Laurie revelled in the new, warm intimacy that mattered as much to her as the sex they had shared because it promised so much for the future with its tender assurance that he hadn't simply wanted her, taken her and dismissed her. Heaven knew what the coming weeks held, but she was suddenly sure that all the barriers had finally come down.

Judd dried her damp curls where the spray of the shower had caught them and gave her one of his own brushes to reduce their tangles. Refusing to let her feel rushed in any way, a much-appreciated sensitivity after such an earth-moving experience, he handed Laurie the items of flimsy underwear, one by one, hooked her bra for her and slipped the thin blouse over her shoulders, taking as much time and as many pains in helping her to dress as he had in undressing her and thus rounding off their recent closeness in a very special way.

'You'll be so late,' Laurie warned, but her tone and her smile held him rather than urged him to hurry away to his meeting.

'Never mind. Mrs Flanagan's future can be decided at a later date. A much more pressing matter needed my attention this morning.' He smiled into shining eyes that seemed to encourage him to go on, but he decided against taking things further at this stage. For surely he had all the time in the world to coax her into a relationship that might lead to the marriage he so desired. 'Friends, Laurie?'

She leaned against his enclosing arm, stifling disappointment that even now he felt unable to offer her anything more than friendship. Don't rush him, an inner voice warned. They had known each only a few weeks, after all. *She* might have known almost at first sight that their destinies were inextricably linked, but men needed rather longer to accept the inevitable.

She kissed him one last time, quick and sweet and slightly shy, for they would revert to being colleagues on his departure, no longer lovers in a wonderful world of their own making, but professionals, doctors with patients to consider and work to be done.

Her mouth soft and slightly swollen from his kisses, her eyes full of memories and her body glowing from the total satisfaction of their love-making, Laurie stood at the window of his room with its tumbled bed and forgotten Hoover and watched his Mercedes roll down the drive, idly registering a familiar splash of colour near the gateway.

She heard the squeal of brakes and saw the car come to a sudden halt, and, fearing an accident, fled from the room and out of the house, hair flying and heart hammering, reaching the scene to find Judd out of the car and glowering.

The woman wasn't hurt. He had seen her and slammed on the brakes in sheer gut reaction to the shock of her presence. As Laurie skidded to a halt, panting and dishevelled, she knew before anything was said that Judd was confronting his ex-wife.

Marla was just as lovely as she had been led to believe. Tall and slim, chestnut hair curling beneath the close-fitting Twenties-style hat and with a skin that positively glowed, she carried herself confidently in her designer-label clothes, very sure of a welcome in spite of her unorthodox and unannounced arrival.

That sureness was in her eyes and voice as she smoothly apologised for stepping out in front of the approaching car. 'I thought you'd seen me, Judd. But I supose you had your mind on your patients, as usual. Or other things, perhaps?'

She shot a mocking glance at Laurie, who hovered and hesitated at a slight distance, unsure whether to go or stay in the light of her recently altered relationship with Judd. His tight-lipped, uncompromising expression was no help to her.

'What the devil are you doing here? I told you when you phoned to stay away!' She had chosen the worst possible moment to surface. His blood still hadn't completely cooled and his body was warm with the imprint of Laurie's touch and scent and sweetness.

The lift of an eyebrow challenged his tone. 'I'm in England for two reasons—to discuss making a film with Tom Cherry and to attend the custody hearing,' Marla told him coolly.

'That doesn't tell me why you're in Umber, on my doorstep.'

She smiled. 'I thought I'd look up some old friends—see all the changes. See Jamie too.' She looked directly into his hardening eyes. 'My son, if you remember.'

'It's taken *you* long enough to remember! The boy hardly knows he has a mother!' Judd's beautiful hands balled into fists and a spasm of black rage swept his handsome face.

Laurie stepped forward in alarm, and he swung to look at her, alerted to her watchful presence. Her obvious distress aroused him to a protective tenderness, and he instantly acted to spare her any of the backlash of the anger and hate that existed between himself and Marla. 'Go back to the house,' he advised tensely. 'There's no reason for you to be involved in any of this!'

Words and tone seemed to exclude her with a hurtful finality, and Laurie's heart quailed as Judd looked at her with the eyes of a stranger. But she stood her ground. 'I don't mean to butt in, but I suggest you come into the house and discuss when it would be convenient for Jamie to see his mother. In private,' she stressed with a meaningful glance at the elderly neighbour who had paused at the gate, ostensibly to catch her breath after climbing the steep hill and to adjust the weight of her loaded basket, but obviously to stand and stare.

Marla looked her over with a flick of contempt in her hard green eyes. 'So this is the woman who's bringing up my son,' she said coldly.

'You haven't lost the habit of jumping to conclusions. Dr Whittaker is a partner in the practice,' Judd retorted harshly, irritated by the instant assumption that he and Laurie were lovers. So they were, but it was none of Marla's business. Their marriage was long dead.

'More than that, surely? She lives with you, I gather.' Marla didn't know why Judd found it necessary to lie. She didn't care how many women he took into his bed or if he married again, except as it affected Jamie. She *did* care about the character and the calibre of any woman who played a part in his upbringing, however, much to her own surprise.

She wasn't a maternal woman. Sheer cussedness had prompted her to oppose Judd's custody application, as well as the idea that it might be good publicity for the coming film if she won her child. Curiosity about the boy had brought her to Umber just before the court hearing, and she hadn't been prepared for the consuming jealousy as she saw Jamie, looking so like Judd, in the company of a woman who was obviously close to him.

Now she studied that same woman with a scornful curl to her lips. Wearing a colourful but inexpensive skirt and blouse, hair tumbling in untidy confusion and bare, brown feet thrust into flat sandals, she looked little more than a child herself, in spite of Judd's assertion that she was a doctor. She had looked more elegant and efficient emerging from the health centre the previous day.

'I live here,' Laurie confirmed. 'But not with Dr Harris.' That was a cherished but unlikely dream.

'That isn't the way I hear it,' Marla said nastily, although she really knew nothing about the situation at Umber House. 'But I'm not concerned with your love-life. I'm only concerned for Jamie's welfare.'

'Rather late in the day,' snarled Judd.

She turned to him. 'I can give him a much better life than he'll ever have in this godforsaken neck of the woods, and my solicitors tell me I have a very good chance of doing so.'

'There's no need for any of this, surely?' Laurie

pleaded, her heart torn by the look in Judd's sombre eyes that betrayed his fear of losing his most precious possession. 'Jamie is the happiest child I know! Judd's done a wonderful job of bringing him up, and Jamie adores him. You did so much harm, caused so much hurt—surely you can't want to destroy them both now?'

'You're a fervent advocate on Judd's behalf, but I really can't feel that Jamie's future is any concern of yours, Dr Whittaker.' Once more Marla challenged Judd. 'I want to talk to Jamie. He's old enough to choose for himself, and he has a right to his options.'

'He's at school,' Laurie told her.

'I'll come back this afternoon when he *isn't* at school,' Marla promised firmly. 'It'll be interesting to find out just how much he knows about his mother.' Her eyes narrowed sharply. 'You weren't stupid enough to let him think I was dead, I hope?'

'Certainly not!' Judd denied angrily.

'Or generous enough to sing my praises, I suppose. No, you wouldn't do that, darling. You're too honest.'

'Jamie has formed his own opinion of his absent mother without anyone's help, believe me!'

Judd's ironic words left Marla in no doubt that it wasn't a flatttering verdict, and her mouth tightened into a thin line. 'Jamie is much too young to have formed any lasting opinions,' she retorted. 'And children forget so easily, don't they? After a few months in Brisbane with me he'll have forgotten all about this place and the people in it. Even his father.'

As she picked a path across the gravel in her extravagantly high heels towards the limousine that edged slowly along the kerb, Judd looked after her with such hatred in his smouldering eyes that Laurie was alarmed.

For he looked capable of murder if he should lose his son to a mean-spirited woman who seemed prompted by jealousy and spite rather than any real love for her child.

CHAPTER TWELVE

LAURIE put a hand on his arm and he covered it with a convulsive clasp of his strong fingers. 'Oh, Judd, why didn't you apply for custody at the time of the divorce?' she mourned softly. It seemed beyond belief that he could have been so remiss or so ill-advised.

Judd brought his gaze from a woman who could never have loved him at all to a woman whose tender, loving heart was in her eyes and touch. 'I didn't think I'd get it. You know as well as I do that custody usually goes to the mother, unless she's morally or mentally unfit—and Marla was neither. What judge would have granted custody of an eight-month-old baby to a busy GP?'

'Why does she want him now? After so long?' queried Laurie.

He shrugged. 'God knows. Unless she thinks having him around might paper over the cracks in her present marriage. Apparently it's in trouble because her husband wants a child and she prefers her career. The same reason why she left me—and she was such an uncaring mother that I honestly thought she'd never come back.'

'But you wanted her back,' Laurie said soberly with a painful catch at her heart.

'Yes, I did. For a long, long time.' There was no

future for him with this warm-hearted, trusting girl unless he was totally honest, Judd knew. 'She was Jamie's mother, and I felt we should be together, a family. That's what marriage is all about, in my book. The divorce went against my innermost feelings, my sense of commitment, and I didn't give up thinking of her as my wife until recently.' Believing Laurie could no longer be in any doubt of the way he felt about her, Judd put an arm round her and rested his cheek on her soft hair. 'Now it's finally finished.'

Laurie wandered back to the house as his car shot away down the hill, knowing it wouldn't be easy for him to concentrate on Mrs Flanagan's problems. But, being the man he was, he would do his best for the determined nonagenarian.

It had been easy to warm to him, to like and admire him, and even easier to love him, and she knew she wanted to spend the rest of her life with Judd—and Jamie.

She wished she could feel that Judd loved her, but so far there had been no reassuring sign of it, she thought wistfully. A sensual man had taken her to bed and uttered a lie that he thought she needed to hear, and she blessed the instinct that had warned her against believing it.

For she was desperately afraid he still loved Marla in spite of everything. Hadn't he told her frankly how much he had cared, how much their marriage had meant to him, and how long he had continued to think of them as a couple even after the divorce? Perhaps he still did, deep down.

Judd collected Jamie from school, allowing him to miss afternoon lessons, and Laurie wondered if he thought Marla might approach the boy if she was given the opportunity.

She had arranged for Edward to take her clinic that afternoon so she could be around to comfort Jamie if he was alarmed by a meeting with an unknown mother. But she soon found that Judd had no intention of allowing Marla near her son.

'I'd be grateful if you'd keep Jamie out of the way for a couple of hours,' he told her in a tone that brooked no argument, and she was perfectly willing to comply.

Her suggestion of a fishing expedition met with the little boy's instant approval. The snaking garden path ran beyond the grounds via a small copse of tall trees and flowering shrubs to a tumbling-down boat-house that was Jamie's favourite place to play whenever he could slip away unobserved.

Laurie understood why Judd was reluctant for his son to enjoy the delights of the river without adult company. The ambling water seemed placid, but there were dangerous currents beneath the surface and numerous clumps of reeds where an adventurous child might become ensnared and drown.

While Jamie fished happily, she sat in an ancient deckchair, one eye on him and the other on her book, content to sit in the sun-dappled shade, reading and dreaming. Birds sang in the trees above their heads and a variety of insects hummed their summer song.

All was still and lovely, and only the unease in

Laurie's heart marred the tranquillity of the scene. For the turn of Jamie's head, the set of his shoulders as he hunched over his rod and the sudden gleam of his smile when he glanced at her, so like Judd's, pierced her with a physical pain.

The man and the boy represented all she could ever want, but Marla's sudden reappearance in their lives had shattered that dream. The woman was no longer a distant shadow but a very real presence that threatened to erode Jamie's loving dependence on her and wreck her newfound relationship with Judd.

She bent her head over her book, forcing the printed word to blot out the black cloud of Jamie no longer needing her and Judd rejecting her because Marla was suddenly back in the frame. Who knew that she hadn't returned for good? If her present marriage was failing, there might be much more to her unexpected presence in Umber than a desire to see the child she had abandoned over six years before.

'You seem to be leading an idyllic existence without me, sweetheart.'

Laurie froze at the unexpted drawl of a familiar voice, her book toppling from her hand. She turned to stare at the man who emerged from the concealment of a huge rhododendron bush.

'How on earth did you get here?' she demanded, not at all pleased to see him.

Cris smiled. 'By car, of course.' He put a light hand on her shoulder and bent to kiss her.

She drew back from that kiss with its tentative tenderness. 'All the way from London?'

'It isn't the far ends of the earth, darling. It just feels like it! Actually, I drove down last night to spend a few days with Mike, and felt I had to look you up.' His eyes were admiring, slightly rueful. 'You look very lovely, Laurie.'

She doubted it. Her skirt and blouse had seen better days and were sadly crumpled from a rough-and-tumble with Jamie before he settled down to fish. Her hair was untidy, a burr or two still clinging to its curls, and she hastily tucked her grubby bare feet out of sight beneath the deck chair, scrabbling for her sandals, struggling to remember why she had once been weak at the knees at the mere sight of him.

There wasn't even the hint of a flutter in her breast as she looked up at Crispin Page. Oh, he was good to look at, a charmer with a smooth tongue and a confidence that usually won him what he wanted. But he was a pygmy compared to Judd, who was a giant of a man in all the ways that really counted!

Fish forgotten, Jamie was looking at Cris with more than a child's natural curiosity in that hard stare, so like his father's, and Laurie felt that the little boy disapproved of that kiss. So did she. She didn't want Cris thinking he could walk back into her life as if he'd never left it!

'Shall I go and get Daddy?' Jamie put down his rod and stood up, evidently feeling she was threatened by the stranger and needed more than his protection.

'It's all right, old man, I'm a friend,' Cris said

confidently. 'No need to worry about me. Besides, the fish are biting.'

Jamie sat down again, doubtful but obedient to the voice of adult authority. 'They aren't really biting,' he muttered, refusing to pretend.

'They will be soon—and I want to talk to Dr Whittaker.' Cris dropped to his haunches beside Laurie and captured both her hands. 'It's so good to see you,' he said softly.

'Is it?' She looked at him doubtfully. Was it pure chance that had brought him to spend a few days with Michael Curtis, or had he hotfooted it to Umber as soon as he heard that she was working and living here? And if so, why?

He took her hands to his lips in a lover-like gesture that was totally unexpected. 'I've missed you, Laurie.'

He sounded so sincere that her heart missed a beat. It would be too ironic if he'd found that he loved her after all now that she had totally fallen out of love with him. She wanted *Judd*! And here was Cris with his smiles and soft words implying that his world had been empty without her in it.

'How did you know where to find me?' She fended off unwelcome sentiments with the prosaic curiosity of her tone.

'I told you. . .Mike! The rest was easy.'

'I mean *now*. Here. . .'

'Someone at the house pointed me in the general direction.'

He could only mean Judd, and her heart plummeted. He had believed for weeks that she was missing Cris when all the time she was falling helplessly in love with him, and now he might suppose she was thrilled to see her former boyfriend again when, in fact, it was the last thing she wanted!

'A red-haired guy,' Cris went on with a query in his voice. 'His daddy, I take it.' He jerked his head at the listening child. 'One of your partners, presumably.'

'I'm not a partner. Not yet.' And might never be now, Laurie thought heavily.

'Then you aren't committed to spending the rest of your life in this social and cultural desert?'

He sounded just like Marla. They would be a perfect pair, both selfish and ambitious and unfeeling! 'No,' she said.

'Thank heavens! Although there are ways round the problem, if you are. There's an opening for a senior surgical registrar at the Northwood, for instance. Shall I apply for the post?'

Laurie stared. 'You'd leave Hartlake—and London—for this social and cultural desert?' Her tone was heavy with irony.

'To be near you—yes!' He said it without hesitation. 'I've been bloody miserable without you all these weeks. I know it's corny, but I didn't know how much you meant until you weren't around any more. And you primed your friends well, didn't you? I didn't know where to start looking for you, until Mike rang and happened to mention seeing you.'

'Cris, I don't understand. . .' She did, of course, and was playing for time, totally bewildered by his rapid change of heart. But was it really any different from the way and the speed with which her own feelings had changed?

'Then I can't be making myself clear. Why don't we go somewhere more private to talk?' He shot a meaningful glance at the silent, solemn little boy who watched them so intently.

Laurie agreed that it was no place for the disappointment she was about to deal him. The sooner she got rid of Cris, the sooner she could get back to the obviously anxious child with the assurance that she had no intention of going away. She knew just what was on Jamie's mind from his expressive blue eyes.

She got to her feet. 'Jamie, I think we'll have to forgo our fish supper,' she said lightly. 'Perhaps you'd like to go and find Daddy while I show my friend where I live.'

He looked puzzled. 'You live here. With me and Daddy.'

'Do you, begod! Mike didn't tell me that part!' Cris exclaimed, his face darkening.

Laurie wondered why people were so quick to leap to conclusions. 'It isn't the way you think, Cris. It's just a convenient arrangement,' she said firmly.

'I bet it is!'

Jealousy must be a unique experience for him, she thought cynically. 'This is my cousin's house and we all share it,' she explained.

'It's Dad's house.'

Checked by the small voice, Laurie spun to look at Jamie in surprise. 'What did you say?'

'It's Dad's house,' he repeated, so surely that there was no room for doubt.

Laurie wondered why Edward hadn't explained properly, even as a number of enigmas fell into place. She had observed that Judd seemed to control the destiny of everyone who lived at Umber House. Now she knew why.

'It doesn't matter whose house it is,' she told the scowling Cris. 'The fact remains that Jamie's father is my cousin's partner in the practice and we're just colleagues.' It was a half-truth, but she didn't want a jealous man accusing Judd of all manner of things and embarrassing everyone.

His expression showed disbelief. 'Damn it, Laurie! Someone or something very special made you leave London in such a hurry!'

'I wanted to get away from you!' There was a snap to her tone, for she had enjoyed her job at Hartlake, loving the work and her small patients, and she would never have left if Cris hadn't played fast and loose with her newly awakened emotions.

Fate had obviously steered her steps to Umber to meet and fall in love with Judd Harris, but as she wasn't sure of a happy ending, she couldn't yet feel it had been a good move.

Cris grinned in obvious delight at the seeming betrayal of the words. 'So I'm very special, am I?'

'Not any more.' Taking Jamie's hand, Laurie headed for the massed rhododendrons that crowded the path to the house.

Cris followed. 'You don't mean that, Laurie,' he

said with his most persuasive smile, a confident hand on her shoulder bringing her to a halt.

His touch and his coaxing tone left her completely cold. For she had just seen Judd, his handsome head thrown back and bright in the sun, his muscles rippling in his broad back and shoulders as he threw a stick across the lawn for Angelo, his deep voice carrying as he shouted encouragement to the dog. Her heart wrenched with a love so strong and so sure that she knew it would last her lifetime and beyond.

She let go of the boy's hand. 'There's Dad, Jamie. . .' She watched him scamper towards his father and hurtle into welcoming arms that swung high and then caught him close in a loving hug. She yearned to be in those strong arms, held safe and much loved, and she wished Cris was a million miles away. 'Oh, Cris, I wish you hadn't come here,' she said helpessly, convinced his presence damaged already dented hopes.

Mistaking the weariness of her tone and the sigh in her voice for a lingering need of him, he promptly put an arm round her and drew her into the concealing bushes. 'I had to come,' he said urgently. 'I care about you.'

He brushed her hair with his lips in a murmuring kiss, oblivious to the resistance in her taut frame. The heavy thud of his heart, the untypical quietness of the words, told Laurie that he was sincere for perhaps the only time in his life.

'It's no use, Cris,' she said, almost wishing they could turn back the clock but knowing it wouldn't make him a man to trust with her heart and her life, a man like Judd. 'It's too late.'

His arms tightened about her possessively. 'How can it be too late?' he demanded fiercely. 'Unless you *are* involved with that kid's father!'

Laurie stiffened. 'We're friends,' she said carefully. 'That's all.' Wasn't that what Judd had said, implying that she shouldn't hope for anything more? 'He has nothing to do with the way I feel. I've changed. I just don't love you any more.' Never had, in truth, but there was no need to plunge the dagger any deeper. She drew out of his arms.

'Not surprising, is it, after the way I behaved?' he said with unexpected humility. 'I can't expect you to throw your arms round my neck and say, yes, Cris, of course I'll marry you—I know I don't deserve that. But I can't believe you're as indifferent as you want me to think, Laurie. I don't believe that all your love for me has melted away completely.'

Laurie wasn't listening. His words fell on deaf ears as the happy tableau of man, boy and dog romping on the sunlit lawn was suddenly shattered.

'Oh, not now, Cris!' she exclaimed impatiently, and hurried to protect Jamie from what must be a traumatic encounter as Marla rounded the corner of the house.

As Judd moved to intercept Marla, cold rage stamped all over him, Laurie dropped to her knees beside the little boy and put her arm round Angelo's neck to restrain him from rushing to greet the newcomer with glad barks and pleased sweeps of his heavy tail.

'We'll have to train you to be a proper guard dog,' she told the wriggling animal, trying to distract Jamie from the scene being enacted behind them as Judd's powerful body blocked the determined woman.

Jamie wasn't easily distracted. He sat back on his heels and looked intently at the arguing couple. 'I know that lady,' he announced.

'It's a long time since you've seen her, Jamie. You were just a baby.' Gently Laurie paved the way.

'She's the lady in the picture,' he insisted.

'What picture, Jamie?'

'The one in Dad's wallet. Is it my mother?'

More evidence that Judd still cared, Laurie thought bleakly. For only a man still deeply in love would carry a photograph of his ex-wife around with him, surely!

'Yes, it is.' She smiled, hugged him. 'All the way from Australia. Isn't that wonderful?'

'My *real* mother?' he persisted.

Laurie nodded. 'She's wanted to come and see you for such a long time, but Australia's a long way. . .' She broke off as Judd stalked angrily towards them, a triumphant Marla at his heels.

Jamie scrambled to his feet, tense and terrified. 'I'm not going with you!' he yelled at his approaching mother, and fled, a wildly barking Angelo behind him, towards the copse and his supposedly secret sanctuary.

No one went after him. That would only alarm him more. Laurie knew Judd would find him later, dry his tears and soothe his fears and promise him that nothing and nobody would ever take him from his father and his home.

Marla turned on Laurie in a fury of frustration. 'What have you been saying to him, damn you?'

'Nothing to alarm him.' She found it impossible to sympathise with this woman who had been rejected by her own child. 'He recognised you and obviously thought you meant to take him away. Running was a natural reaction, in the circumstances. You may be his mother, but you're a total stranger to Jamie.'

'Recognised?' Judd echoed. 'But how? He was just a baby!'

'Apparently he's seen a photo. . .' Laurie looked away from penetrating eyes that might see the collapse of all her dearest dreams in her own.

As she turned away, leaving them to settle the problem of Jamie's behaviour between them, she saw the slight, instinctive movement of his hand towards a back trouser pocket that held his wallet with its memento of happier and still hankered-after days and knew that Jamie hadn't been mistaken.

The mistake was hers for foolishly hoping she could replace the absent Marla in his heart and life.

Cris still stood at the edge of the shrubbery, watching and wondering. 'What was that about?' he asked curiously, his gaze riveted on the beautiful woman in her striking scarlet outfit.

'Just a family argument.' And they *were* still a family in spite of the divorce. Once they had loved and lived together in a marriage that had produced Jamie, a bond between them that could never be broken. He might even be the cement that would eventually weld them again.

'Dour chap, isn't he? No manners at all that I noticed,' Cris said critically.

'Oh, dear, was he rude to you?' Laurie recalled her own first impressions of Judd, so soon replaced by more favourable ones.

'Let's just say that I had a warmer welcome from the dog.'

Laurie smiled. 'Oh, Angelo loves visitors.' She tucked a hand into his arm and drew him towards the house, the first move in steering him out of her life forever. 'I talked a lot about my cousin Edward, didn't I? I'd like you to meet him, and he may be back from surgery now.'

She didn't really want the men to meet, encouraging Edward as well as Judd to think that she wanted to pick up the threads of a former romance, but nor did she want to linger with Cris in the dense shrubbery with its overtones of clandestine meetings.

'I didn't come all this way to meet your cousin,' Cris objected, swinging her round to face him. 'I want things settled. I need to know where I stand.'

Laurie didn't think she *could* have made it any plainer! But his characteristic confidence made him blind and deaf and resistant towards the mere idea of failure, she realised wearily.

As she hesitated, seeking the right words to convince him that it was over, he swept her into his arms and held her firmly. Laurie looked over his shoulder into Judd's enigmatic eyes as he rounded the thickly foliaged bush that had concealed his approach and their seeming embrace. The striking blue of his eyes abruptly hardened to sombre steel.

Laurie hastily freed herself. 'Cris is an old friend from Hartlake.' It sounded lame to her own ears.

'So I understand.' Judd's smile gave no sign of his wrenching dismay. He had no claim on Laurie, but that didn't stop him from wanting to pummel the fellow to a pulp. 'I'm looking for Jamie. I've persuaded Marla to give me time to talk to him. The boy's had a shock, and I'm entirely to blame. I should have prepared him.' As he strolled on, he added over his shoulder, 'By the way, Marcus is on the mend, apparently. So don't hesitate to do what you want to do, Laurie. You won't be leaving anyone in the lurch.'

It seemed to Laurie's sensitive heart that he hadn't minded the sight of her in another man's arms and wouldn't care if she went away and he never saw her again.

'I don't know why I thought he was a rival,' said Cris with a relieved laugh. 'The guy doesn't even like you, does he?'

Laurie didn't answer, struggling to master the tidal wave of anguish that drowned her dreams.

CHAPTER THIRTEEN

THEY had taken only a few steps when Laurie heard Judd calling Jamie and realised that the boy hadn't taken refuge in his usual hiding-place. It seemed he didn't want to be found, and who could blame him? It might always have been a deep-seated fear that his mother would come to claim him one day. Children stored up half-heard and half-understood remarks and built up anxieties that suddenly erupted into terror.

'I must help to find Jamie,' she said abruptly. 'Go back to Mike's place, and I'll ring you later, Cris.'

She didn't copy Judd and call Jamie, alerting him. Instead, she checked all his secret places, hunting among the trees and under the bushes, peering through heavy foliage and breaking through bracken and bramble that caught at her hair and skirt and scratched spitefully at her bare arms and legs.

Intent on his own affairs, Angelo padded past her in pursuit of some small, swift animal that he would never catch and was too soft-hearted to harm if he did.

Steadily Laurie moved further from the house, sure that Jamie knew she was near and eluding her, darting from one bolt-hole to the next, turning it into a game and forgetting his fears.

As she emerged into open ground and bright

sunlight near the water's edge, she glimpsed the blue of his shorts as he scrambled into the shelter of the reeds. Relieved, she crept stealthily closer, but his keen boy's ear caught the rustle of a step and the snap of a twig and he backed even further into the reeds.

Laurie's warning cry coincided with the splash as he toppled backwards into the foaming river.

It was a huge joke to Jamie, but she couldn't bear to think of his small body being swiftly sucked under and trapped in the massed reeds and not being found until too late. Fortunately, she had been on hand to throw herself face down and plunge both arms into the water to snatch at him, getting a good handful of his shorts and hauling him back to the bank.

Giggling and squirming, water streaming from his hair and clothes, he buried his face against her breast as she hugged him close, thankful that he hadn't come to any harm but for a few mouthfuls of brackish water.

'Oh, Jamie, you gave me such a scare!' It wasn't a scold. Her heart was too full for anger.

'You chased me. I was only hiding. . .'

Judd appeared at a run, having heard her cry from a distance, a look on his face that Laurie hoped never to see again. He dropped to his knees beside them and threw his arms round them both, hugging and rocking and murmuring heartfelt relief, for there had been a dreadful moment as he rounded the bend and saw them in a crumpled heap on the riverbank when his heart had hit rock bottom.

'I'm all right, Dad,' Jamie said stoutly, struggling

to prise them apart as he came close to being crushed between them.

'He's just wet,' Laurie confirmed with a shaky laugh, seeing the colour return to Judd's face as he leaned away from them. 'He was backing away from me and slipped. Luckily I was close enough to grab him. . .'

'And save his life,' Judd said soberly.

'I *can* swim, Dad!' It was an indignant protest that overlooked Jamie's panic as he hit the water and completely forgot how to do the few strokes of dog-paddle he had so proudly displayed in the local swimming pool only a few days previously.

'I know you can, son. But the river isn't the place to practise. I've warned you a thousand times about the currents!'

'No harm done, Judd.' Laurie put a gently warning hand on his arm as she saw Jamie's crestfallen face. 'He'll be more careful in future, I'm sure.' As Judd took Jamie from her arms in a protective, thankful embrace, she scrambled to her feet. 'Let's get him into the bath—and he'll need something to take that nasty taste of river out of his mouth,' she added meaningfully.

Judd nodded. 'I've just the thing to kill off all the tadpoles you've probably swallowed as well as any bugs,' he declared with a lightness that belied the seriousness of the matter.

'Yuk!' Jamie shuddered, grinning, obviously none the worse for his adventure.

Serene was in the kitchen, preparing tea for the children, and she instantly took charge with the quiet efficiency that seemed able to cope with any crisis that didn't concern her own offspring. She whisked Jamie off to a bath, while Judd went for his medical bag and the tablets to counteract the impurities of the water and Laurie went to change out of her damp and muddy clothes.

She was pottering in her small kitchen when she heard a light tap on the sitting-room door and looked out to see Judd. 'Come in. I'm just making tea.' She smiled at him. 'My prescription for all ills.'

Judd lowered his lean frame into a chair to the homely chink of teacups, the rattle of teaspoons, and relaxed now that Jamie, bathed and dressed in clean clothes and watching a favourite TV programme with Jenefer, really seemed none the worse. He didn't seem to realise his brush with death, while Judd still shook and trembled inside with the dread inspired by the incident.

He could never repay his debt to the girl who moved quietly between kitchen and cosy sitting-room with the tea-tray, and assortment of small cakes and biscuits, and a flow of small talk that didn't require or expect answers. He owed her more than his son's life. He had Laurie to thank for a whole new approach to the future and the final demise of the past.

It was pleasant to sit in her comfortable room with its various indications of her tenancy—some delicate porcelain figurines, a slender crystal vase with its wild flowers, presumably picked and presented by the children, a coiled stethoscope peeping from her medical bag, a magazine and a half-written letter on a table, a pair of shoes kicked off and left to lie. . . perhaps she wasn't the tidiest girl in the world, but she was warmly human and very feminine, and he loved her very much.

Laurie curled up on the sofa with her feet beneath her, looking pretty and youthful in powder-pink trousers and striped pink shirt. 'How's Jamie now?' she asked.

Judd smiled ruefully. 'Not even subdued! He thinks it was amusing. Just as well, perhaps. But I shall never be able to thank you enough, Laurie.'

'I only did what anyone would have done,' she demurred. 'Nothing spectacular or dangerous. I didn't even go into the water after him!'

'So I can't offer you any of my special pills to kill off the tadpoles?' It was easier to make light of the incident than to stress its dark side.

'Yuk!' she echoed Jamie, and they both laughed.

He leaned towards her, sobering. 'Isn't there an old Chinese proverb that says if you save a life then that life belongs to you?'

Laurie's smile was misty. 'I wish he *was* mine. . .' She lightened the moment before she blurted all the other sentiments that crowded her heart. 'I'd adopt him, but I don't think his father would part with him!'

'Well, he's certainly adopted *you*! You mean a lot to Jamie and he's going to miss you very much, I'm afraid.' Judd exploited his son's needs quite shamelessly, unable to use his own heartfelt need of Laurie to persuade her to stay in Umber.

'That sounds as if you really believe Marla will win custody,' she said in alarm.

'I've no real fears on that score. . .and it puzzles me that she challenged my application, in view of some doubtful facts that have come to light and which she must have known couldn't be concealed once she tried to get custody of Jamie. She took drugs after she left me and spent some time in a rehabilitation clinic in Sydney. She may or may not be completely cured, but the judge will consider her to be an unfit mother, in the circumstances—or so my solicitor assures me. I told her so this afternoon, and advised her to go back to Brisbane and forget she ever had a son. Just as she's done so successfully for the past six years.'

Laurie's heart quickened. For surely he couldn't speak about Marla with such cold contempt if he still cared anything for her?

'Then what did you mean? About Jamie missing me? I'm not planning to leave.' It was carefully light.

'Not at the moment, perhaps. But I imagine you mean to go back to London in the New Year. General practice isn't really what you want to do, is it?'

Judd left unsaid his fear that it would be her heart and not her professional preferences that took her away from Umber, feeling he had no right to speak about her on-off-on again romance.

'I've worked hard at it!' Laurie sat up to glower at him indignantly. 'Whenever I've been allowed to do the job I came here to do!'

It was a tart reminder that she seemed to have

spent more of her time coping with the domestic situation at Umber House than practising medicine!

'Indeed you have,' soothed Judd. 'But being a GP takes total commitment, and half the time your mind seems to have been on other things.' Hankering for Page, he almost added, stifling a painful jealousy.

Laurie could scarcely admit that half the time her mind had been on *him*! It was so unprofessional!

'Dirty dishes, dirty shirts,' she agreed sardonically. 'I really haven't had much chance to find out if I like being a GP. But I've no plans to give it up, unless you and Edward decide not to invite me to become a partner in the practice!'

'I thought you and Page had other plans for the future,' Judd said slowly, ploughing a hand through the bronze thatch of his hair in a way that betrayed the inner conflict between hope and caution.

'*He* may have plans. It doesn't mean that I'm interested in anything he has to suggest,' Laurie said firmly.

Judd's face lightened. 'I'm glad to hear it.' He smiled at her suddenly. 'I'd miss you too, Laurie.'

Heart and senses confused by the warming blaze in his beautiful eyes, almost afraid to believe what she read in their depths, she leaned forward to indicate his empty cup. 'More tea?'

'No, thanks.' He looked at her with thoughtful eyes. 'Is it really over between you and Page?'

'It was over weeks ago.' The moment I looked into your eyes and toppled into the fathomless depths of loving you, Laurie added silently.

'Then, if you really mean to stay, I've a proposition to put to you, Laurie.' More than one, but Judd warned himself not to rush his fences. It might still be too soon to admit that he loved and needed her and wanted her to marry him.

Her heart shook. 'Go ahead.' She smiled at him with tremulous encouragement.

'You may remember my proposal for a small trauma unit, privately funded and run by local GPs. I think you were at a meeting when it was mentioned, off the record, much to Gwen Beavis's disgust. She doesn't approve of private medicine.'

'Yes, I remember,' said Laurie. But what could it have to do with the hope that had transfixed her heart, a hope instantly dashed by the practicality of his tone?

'I'd like you to play a prominent part in helping me set it up. I know you're a paediatrician, but you're very good with the elderly, and a fair number of our patients will fall into that category. We shall treat children too, obviously. I'm hoping to include a physiotherapy unit for cerebral palsy and stroke victims, and I'm pretty sure I'll get NHS support for that venture, at least.'

'Sounds exciting,' said Laurie.

'It could be,' said Judd. 'If we both work at it.'

She looked at him quickly, detecting a *double entendre*, and met the warm promise in his smiling eyes. Her heart soared, but she still didn't dare to believe what she was seeing in those dark blue depths.

He reached to link her slender wrist with strong fingers, delighting in the sheer silk of her skin and detecting the hurrying pulse with much more than professional interest. 'Laurie. . .?'

She couldn't cope with the sudden flood of feeling, the agonising fear that she might be misreading the look in his eyes. Didn't he know how her heart trembled at his touch, how much it hurt to love and want so much, how tempted she was to slip into arms that might not really want to hold her except in brief, meaningless passion?

Panicking, Laurie leaped to her feet and hurried to the window as a low rumble of thunder in the distance gave her an excuse to distance herself from his overwhelming nearness.

'There's a storm coming—just look at that purple sky!'

She widened the open casement, needing to cool her flushed cheeks and calm her tumultuous emotions, but there was little air about and everything was hushed, the hum of insects and the song of the birds silenced by nature's threatening stillness.

Not a breath of air stirred the trees, and as she looked down to the garden, she saw the drowsing Angelo stir and lumber to his feet and pad towards the house as he sensed the impending rain.

Judd moved to stand behind her, bending to look at the ominous heavens. The first flash of lightning streaked the lowering sky with vivid blue and white, and Laurie winced and drew back, colliding with him.

Instantly his arms enfolded her and he turned her to face him, looking down at her with an intensity of longing in his eyes. 'I love you so much, Laurie,' he said tensely. 'It may be too soon to suggest it, but I want you to marry me. Will you?'

She gasped with delight as the thunderbolt of the words registered. 'Oh, Judd! Are you *sure*? Do you mean it? Do you really, truly love me?' she demanded breathlessly, daring at last to feel that a long and lasting happiness was within her reach.

Judd took her lovely face in both strong hands and kissed her, a long and deeply satisfying kiss that left her in absolutely no doubt that her love for him was returned in full measure.

'If you aren't convinced now then I *am* out of practice when it comes to loving,' he teased softly, and she leaned her head on his broad shoulder with a sigh of content.

'Jamie will be so pleased,' she said happily. Then, as a thunderclap broke above Umber House to coincide with another streak of electric lightning, she began to draw away. 'I ought to go to him, Judd. You know how much he hates storms.'

His arms held her still and very close to his heart, the place she was destined to occupy for the rest of his life. 'I need you more than Jamie does right now,' he told her with the masterful tones of a lover, and kissed her again.